Sign up for book announcements and special deals at:

AWBALDWIN.COM

Copyright 2022 by A.W. Baldwin

ISBN   978-1-7353626-7-0 Hardbound
ISBN   978-1-7353626-8-7 Paperback
ISBN   978-1-7353626-9-4 ebook

Cover art by Daniel Thiede.

For Nelson, Al, and all my other friends and colleagues with the Northern Arapaho Tribe

and

For Baldwin, Crocker, & Rudd, P.C., and all the wonderful folks who make it a special place to be

"This harrowing techno-thriller is an impressive achieve-ment – timely, and rich with research, intrigue, and a main character you will be rooting for from the be-ginning all the way to the exhilarating climax. Highly recommended!"

"The chemistry between Harry and Keaton is electrify-ing." "…there is never a dull moment…The Antidote [is] a gripping novel."

THE ANTIDOTE

A.W. BALDWIN

Broken Inn

The mob, undercover agents, and secret payloads make *Broken Inn* a dangerous place for a fresh reporter, a newspaper photographer, and a moonshining hermit.

"The desert bakes while the danger scorches in another outstanding mystery from A.W. Baldwin."
– *#1 New York Times Bestselling Author Dirk Cussler.*

Winner of awards from the Grand Master Adventure Writer's Competition, New York City Big Book Awards, Independent Press Awards, Global Book Awards, and Books Shelf Writing Awards.

Wings Over Ghost Creek

Can a moonshining hermit, a reluctant pilot, and a misfit student uncover the truth and escape an archeology field class that hides assassins and dealers in black-market treasure?

A page-turning thriller where the landscape is beguiling, the villains wicked, and the action non-stop."
– *New York Times #1 Bestselling author Dirk Cussler*

Baldwin has a "gift for capturing the reader's attention at the beginning and keeping them spellbound"
– *Onlinebookclub.org* review.

Winner of awards from the Grand Master Adventure Writer's Competition and Global Book Awards; Reader's Favorite Five Star Review.

Raptor Canyon

Armed with a full box of toothpicks (and a little dynamite), can a moonshining hermit, a big-city lawyer, and a student with secret ties to the site monkey-wrench a corrupt land deal and recast the fate of Raptor Canyon?

"A gem of a read…"
– *#1 New York Times best-selling author Dirk Cussler*

"[You'll be] holding your heart and your breath at the same time…"
– *Peter Greene, award winning author of The Adventures of Jonathan Moore series*

"A hoot of an adventure novel…"
– *Reader's Favorite.*

Grand Master Adventure Writer's Finalist Award and Screencraft Cinematic Book Contest Semi-finalist; Reader's Favorite Five Star Review.

Diamonds of Devil's Tail

When diamonds appear in a remote canyon stream, whitewater rafters and artifact thieves set off in a deadly race to the source.

"Relic is a unique and intriguing character...passionately interested in preserving the ancient archeological sites and conserving the land and water...[We] enthusiastically recommend it to readers who enjoy thrillers, action-packed adventure, and crime novels."
– *Onlinebookclub.org* four out of four Star Review.

"Another rollicking Relic ride from A.W. Baldwin...a bunch of double-crossing, dirt dealing, diamond thieves run into Relic's trademark wit and ingenuity. Enjoy!"
– Jacob P. Avila, *Cave Diver.*

"...an adeptly written thriller...the excitement and tension are superb...the entire plot [is] compelling"
– *Readers' Favorite Five Star Review.*

Desert Guardian

A moonshining hermit; a campus bookworm; a midnight murder. Can an unlikely duo and a whitewater crew save themselves and an ancient Aztec battlefield from deadly looters?

Desert Guardian is an "engaging action… mystery" with "tough, credible characters."
— *Reader's Favorite Five Star Review*.

Buy now from a bookstore near you or amazon.com

For more about these award-winning books go to:
AWBALDWIN.COM

CHAPTER 1

A single cloud arose in the pale, blank sky – a vision born from the invisible. Dr. Blackstone knew that the intersection of warm, moist air and colder currents caused the cloud to arise from the void, but the creation of such living, swirling motion never ceased to amaze him.

It was almost as amazing as his discovery, also risen from the void.

It had come about nearly by accident.

He'd experimented with mustard seeds, grains of wheat and rice, and, on a whim, seeds from a small tree native to North America: a wild berry-producing workhorse with little economic value. But the seeds, God bless them, responded to low-level radiation like no other, producing DNA mutations of a remarkable variety. He'd been searching for ways to decrease the toxicity of the leaves and increase the size of the berries. By chance, one mutation altered the plant's absorption of gases in ways he would never have predicted. It had taken him nearly six full years to replicate and isolate the desirable DNA from the pool. A unique seed from that plant produced one with leaves and roots that now could change the history of planet Earth herself.

Blackstone patted his pockets, his knees flexing with a nervous, buoyant energy. He'd earned his doctorate in botany nearly forty years before, when he'd focused on historic genetic engineering – a study of how Native Americans had developed corn into a highly productive crop, now the source of nearly seventy percent of the carbon that's in every living citizen. Since then, the discovery of DNA and the development of tools to enhance specific properties had exploded as a science of its own. Still, public reticence about consuming genetically engineered plants seemed to dampen funding for research. Blackstone had cobbled together three different sources for his own projects – two small university grants and one larger one from the U.S. Department of Agriculture. In fact, USDA representative Wayland Jones was due to arrive in about thirty minutes.

Blackstone unlocked the front door. The faint scent of sandalwood and hay seeped through his office, a single-story Indiana farmhouse renovated seven years ago. The old living room, bedroom, and dining hall had been converted into a single, large area. A sink, refrigerator, and propane stove lined the far wall, remnants from the original kitchen. The hardwood floor creaked as he walked to his desk, one of two messy workspaces on the south side of the building. He set his leather satchel on the floor and moved to a coffee maker by the sink. He checked to make sure that fresh, ground beans were in the container, added water, and turned on the machine. A row of old high school lockers formed a wall between the main room and the back door. Six were empty, but the groundskeeper used one locker and Blackstone's summer assistant, Lila, used another.

His thoughts returned to the seeds. He'd verified his test results the day before yesterday and hurried home to leftover spaghetti and a bottle of chianti. He was an established bachelor, but he had to tell someone, so he called his friend Fanny, an old schoolmate on whom he'd had a momentous crush, now a scientist he could trust to verify his discovery. He'd tried three separate times but gotten only her answering machine. He'd left a message about what she would get from him in the mail and that he needed her assistance in deciding just what to do with it.

You didn't drop this kind of discovery on the world without some help.

After he'd given up on Fanny, he'd called Jones to share his news. Jones was neither a friend nor a colleague but a bureaucrat who checked boxes on a clipboard for the government. Still, Jones had monitored his work with some interest, and he'd have to tell the USDA about the discovery sooner or later. After a glass and a half of chianti, he'd told some of it to Jones – about the unusual trait he'd noticed, the DNA isolation, the incorporation into a healthy plant, yesterday's test results. Not specifically which plants were involved, but enough to pique his interest. Jones had listened closely, asking sensible questions. He told Blackstone that his funding agreement required confidentiality; that he could not reveal his study or test results without prior approval from the USDA. After all, the discovery could have national security implications. Blackstone doubted that was true, but he would re-read the grant conditions about keeping data confidential. And grant conditions be damned, he was sharing his results with Fanny – she could perform the required peer review. And of course, Lila already knew some of what he was working on. He'd tell her the rest when she came to work this morning – she would certainly celebrate the news with him.

News, indeed.

Blackstone's seeds would be the talk of the town, the achievement of a lifetime, his ticket to funding for another decade if he wanted that much. Or maybe he would hit the talk show circuit, write a best-selling book, and retire to a beach somewhere... Such fanciful thoughts!

He released a guffaw.

The coffee machine sputtered and prompted his memory. "Before I forget..." He went through the back door and crossed an open area to a permanent greenhouse where he grew his research plants. He unlocked the door and moved quickly inside to a row of large bushes.

A one-gallon plastic bag filled with leaves and seeds sat next to one of the plants. He reached for a pad of paper and pencil, scribbled a note, then folded and tucked the message into the plastic bag.

He turned and carried the bag into the office and placed it into Lila's locker. She would ship it to Fanny.

He walked back outside, crossing the ground to the greenhouse.

A single, sharp crack pierced the air.

His back shoved violently forward and, in that split second, he thought that lightening must have struck him, one billion joules of energy charring his spine. He spun helplessly into the dirt, his eyes aimed into the pale sky, and he searched, but there was no cumulonimbus, no thunderstorm, no source for a bolt of electricity.

Another cloud arose from nothingness in the vacant, morning blue, growing, swirling itself into existence, and he knew undeniably that it was the most beautiful and final thing he would see in his lifetime.

CHAPTER 2

"I'm going to be late at being early," Lila scolded herself. She pulled her hair into a tight ponytail and glanced at the mirror. Rich, brown eyes stared back at themselves, framed with black lashes, and she gave herself a crooked smile. No makeup for the greenhouse girl.

Lila had been born in Toronto, but her mother's parents had been Americans. She'd visited Grandpa and Grandma regularly in their backwoods home south of Manistee, Michigan, where they'd kept two saddle horses, Spots and Vic, a pair of hyperactive English setters, and a dozen chickens carefully penned away from the dogs. She'd spent holidays and two full summers with them – so much of her youth that she considered herself both American and Canadian in equal measure.

When Lila had heard about a botany scholarship at the University of Indiana, she'd sought an F-1 student visa to study in the United States – it was like stepping into her own back yard. She'd found a great summer job this year, but it was way off-campus. Under the terms of her visa, she needed pre-approval from the university. She hadn't realized her mistake until last week, when she spoke with a friend from Australia who had a similar problem and had nearly been deported. Now Lila had to ask for permission retroactively. It seemed like such a silly rule, really. But last semester, two exchange students had had their visas revoked just for missing their appointments with USCIS, the U.S. Citizenship and Immigration Services. One of the students had been taken into custody by ICE, Immigration and Customs Enforcement, and summarily removed from the country.

The United States took immigration and visa issues very seriously.

She planned to visit with USCIS tomorrow afternoon to seek forgiveness – and permission – to finish her final year of study. Surely, they wouldn't deport her for such a simple oversight, would they? She would ask her boss, Dr. Blackstone, for a letter of support this morning. A man of his credentials and experience ought to influence the USCIS in her favor.

She left her tiny apartment and set a bowl of cream outside her door for Abbey, a stray calico who'd adopted most of the tenants in the re-modelled boarding house. As spectral as she was clairvoyant, Abbey materialized in the hallway, padding toward the milky treat.

Lila knelt to the hardwood floor. "To stray or not to

stray? That is the question, eh, Abbey?"

The calico murmured in appreciation, arching her back against Lila's hand. As an only child, she had long felt a kinship with animals and, yes, with the plants she cared for.

She stood, pulled her daypack onto her shoulders, and hurried down the stairs. She hopped on her bike for the ride to work, an "office" in an old farmhouse with a large nursery in the back acre. She'd declared her major in botany at the close of spring semester and gotten permission to take a couple of graduate-level courses in plant oxygenation. She'd found the summer job with Dr. Blackstone, a quirky old botanist with some off-the-wall projects in "agricultural architecture." He'd been tinkering with low-level radiation to promote DNA mutations then studying them in efforts to enhance the natural properties of a host of plants. She knew he was excited about recent gas absorption tests, and the anticipation had been contagious. She decided to arrive before 8:00 this morning to talk with him about it, but now she was running late for her plan to be early.

Maybe she'd make it exactly on time.

She pedaled easily along the streets of Bluejacket, a small town southeast of Terre Haute named after a military leader of the Shawnee in the 1700s, a predecessor of Tecumseh. A late August cold snap had turned the leaves of the old ash tree on Library Corner to a blushing shade of yellow. She turned onto Grange-Hall, a country road where the terrain dipped on a gentle slope toward the farm. Cottonwoods lined the western edge of the road. A driveway curved away from the pavement, narrowed, and turned to light gravel. She rode it around the last bend and stopped at the front porch.

Dr. Blackstone's blue Toyota pickup was parked along the side of the building. A grey Pontiac sedan sat next to it, vaguely familiar to her. Maybe Dr. Blackstone had invited Mr. Jones, the USDA representative, to the project this morning.

She hopped two steps up the porch and went quickly into the office. The area was empty – the others were probably in the greenhouse. Blackstone's desk seemed in more disarray than usual, but it was always a bit of a mess. The smell of fresh coffee reached her nose, drawing her to it. She pulled a mug from the shelf, poured herself a cup, and left it on the counter to cool. She moved past the end of the lockers that formed a hallway separating the back door, and part of the kitchen, from the office. The exit behind her led to a grassy area outside and the nursery beyond. She set her pack on the floor.

She opened her locker and found on the middle shelf a gallon bag full of seeds and a few fresh leaves. She could see a folded note inside, a name and address pressed against the clear plastic. It must be something Dr. Blackstone wants her to mail today. She placed the bag inside her daypack, atop a small pair of shears, and zipped it shut.

She took a tentative sip of hot coffee and thought she heard something just beyond the back door. Drink in hand, she turned, opened the door, and peered outside.

Dr. Blackstone lay on the cool grass thirty feet away, eyes fixed on the sky.

Something was terribly wrong.

She stepped out, dropped her mug into the dirt, and rushed to Blackstone's side, skidding to the ground on her knees.

His pupils were unnaturally large, his face frozen in calm surrender.

As she realized what she was seeing, her anxiety deepened, furrowing into itself, sucking the heat from her skin.

"Oh, my god!" she shook his shoulder once, then again. "Dr. Blackstone, doctor, doctor, are you..." Her words withered, too feeble to find their way out of her throat.

Blood leaked beneath his shoulders, and she knew the worst was true.

She leapt to her feet and spun back toward the farmhouse, driven to call for help, her knee banging against the doorframe, toes stumbling over the threshold. She caught her balance and began to step around her pack, but something blocked the light from the kitchen.

Wayland Jones stood in her path, ten feet away, his shirt disheveled, his face red from exertion. He balanced a stack of files under each arm, manila folders slipping out of his grasp.

"Blackstone!" she shouted, pointing behind her.

"I just called 911," Jones spoke in a whispered rush, "but whoever did this is still here, Lila."

Still here. It took a moment for the meaning to settle in. Jones took a step toward her.

She stole a breath, reached for her pack, and turned back to the open doorway. She tried not to look at her boss again, but she couldn't help taking one final glance at his slackened face, his sad, limp form crumpled in the grass.

Lila sprinted across the open ground until she passed the entrance and the edge of the greenhouse, where she spun behind the building. She listened for the sound of Jones behind her, or the killer, or anyone at all, but the unbreathing air offered only an eerie hush. She stood absolutely still.

She peeked around the edge but saw no living human.

She turned, clenching her teeth, then shouldered her pack, running as fast as her legs could carry her, past the greenhouse, away, away toward the woods that separated the farmhouse from civilization and whoever had killed her harmless, quirky, doctor.

CHAPTER 3

"Lose something?" Harry tugged against his white hair, tightening the band on his ponytail, and watched his friend.

A left-over smell of gasoline tainted the air in Johnny's garage. Brackets and screws and bolts cluttered a workbench that ran across the back wall. Johnny lifted a box of nails, slid a hammer aside, and ran his fingers along the back of the workspace. Gray hair perfectly groomed, he was thin as a stickman drawing and sharp as a tiger's tooth, his walnut eyes quick and shiny as glitter. Johnny turned and peered at him from under his brow. "Old GPS beacon. Had it here somewhere…" He shrugged absent-mindedly, a crooked grin on his lips. "Good to see you. So…have you thought it over?" Johnny had presented him with a business proposal.

Harry looked down at his scuffed-up boots, considering the deal. He still owed Johnny $6,000 on loan.

"This would make us even?"

"Better than that."

"Right."

Johnny smiled and reached toward him, pointing with an open hand. "Hey, remember that time we got busted on the football field? Waiting to meet up with Bailey and Amber?"

"Nearly busted," Harry corrected him.

"That's right, nearly busted. You talked that school cop in circles so long he finally let us go with just a warning – and I had a dime bag in my back pocket!" Johnny shook his head. "Man, if he'd have searched us that night…"

"Yeah, close call. Course, the girls never showed…" Harry shook his head. The two of them had been known for skipping class and drinking cheap wine down by the river.

But they weren't in high school anymore.

Johnny wanted Harry to deliver forty pounds of premium marijuana to another dealer in east Texas, a place just south of Guadalupe National Park. Pot was still illegal in Indiana, Texas, and most places in between, and small growers could make some decent money through direct sales to customers. Harry would earn ten percent. Six of it would be used to repay Johnny, leaving Harry with $6,000 in cash.

Seed money for his dream of opening a local bookstore.

He'd gotten a degree in English, but other than

employment at Indiana State University as an assistant librarian, he'd never relied much on the degree. He'd married while in college, but they never had any children, and when his wife passed away, he'd needed a change of careers. He became a paralegal, worked for a law firm for years, then claimed his social security and returned to work in the library part-time.

Literature was a hobby, not a career, but he'd nurtured the idea of owning a bookshop for decades.

He remembered one of his favorite bookstores, a crowded Spanish Colonial home seeped in the smells of parchment and pipe tobacco. The bookshelves were built so high you had to use a ladder to reach the upper rows – a place to explore, both physically and mentally, a place to gorge his mind beyond what it could consume. He'd promised to limit himself at every visit, pledging to buy no more than four books at a time. He'd failed as often as he'd succeeded.

Johnny's pot would join the flow of commerce and Harry would get the funding he needed to set up his shop. He would search for just the right house in just the right location, live in the basement or the attic and live on ramen noodles if he had to. He smiled to himself. Once it became legal, he could expand the business to sell pot cookies and brownies, too.

To help cover travel expenses, Johnny had also offered $500 now and another five on delivery. Harry already had a road trip lined up for that same part of

Texas – that was what had prompted Johnny's proposition. He could make the run for Johnny at no extra cost and earn a solid paycheck for the effort. But he'd be carrying $120,000 worth of illegal pot across seven different states. Despite the country's changing attitudes, if he was caught, Harry could still spend years of his precious life in jail.

Harry's other friend, Keaton, was a separate issue.

Keaton had his own reason to travel to Texas and had invited Harry to help drive the freeways and keep him company. For his own protection, Keaton didn't need to know about the marijuana.

Harry would keep him out of this deal with Johnny.

Shoving aside a hint of lingering doubt, Harry looked at Johnny and nodded. "Where, exactly, do I deliver it?"

Johnny smiled a row of ivory teeth and handed Harry a note with a name and address. He pounded on a door that led from the garage into his house and shouted: "Guys!"

Harry had never liked Johnny's two associates.

A rangy dude in his forties named Cole stepped into the garage. The man's eyes spread wide beneath his brow, two bulging blue orbs that Harry expected to swivel independently, like those lizards that licked their own faces. His chin split with a deep dimple, his lips a line in the sand. Rumor was he'd drowned a man once, in Cagles Mill Lake, east of Terre Haute. Though it had never been proven, Harry didn't doubt it.

A hulk of a man called Meatball followed Cole into the garage, mean as a splinter in your ass. A rounded belly bulged against his yellow shirt, a dollop of unkempt hair balanced atop his head. Said to be from the rough side of Cincinnati, the man's expression was as dense as river mud.

Cole and Meatball helped Johnny with local sales and deliveries but thought much too highly of themselves, playing "muscle" for an operation that seldom needed it. Johnny would be far better off without them.

They each carried an identical green dry bag about two feet in diameter and four feet tall. Rubberized material rolled tightly at the top kept the bags waterproof. A small lock held each top in place. Shoulder straps allowed them to be carried like a backpack.

"Here are the keys." Johnny raised them in display for Harry. "They're not for security; they're to show the buyer the bags have not been tampered with. I'll mail one of the keys to him."

"Got it."

"You get the other one..." Johnny's voice dropped an octave, a quick message tucked inside: don't screw with me, old friend.

Johnny stepped back and patted one of the bags. "Each of these has a GPS locator beacon inside, right on top. My guys and I can monitor their location anywhere in the world from a laptop with a simple access code. A good businessman protects his investment, you know." He narrowed his eyes. "If you vary too much from the route, I'll be on the phone to make sure you're OK, all right?"

Harry nodded.

"You're sure that old car of Keaton's will make it?"

"Sure as any. It's a classic, but it's solid."

"Call if you have any trouble." Johnny handed him an envelope of cash.

"No worries, man." Harry tucked the envelope into his back pocket without counting it.

He knew Johnny was trusting him, too.

CHAPTER 4

It's a bit of a time machine, Keaton thought – an extra slice of the fourth dimension. He stepped back to get a better look.

Deep-water blue on the body, pale blue on the rooftop, the 1960 Chevrolet Bel Air seemed less like a car and more like a spaceship from the days of love beads and psychedelics. Windswept lines curved from her grill then straight back to a pair of horizontal ledges that reminded him of the fins on a ballistic rocket. Below that, chrome shaped like a jet airplane, complete with a silver contrail, ran from the middle of the rear door panel all the way to the back bumper.

His uncle Rodger had bequeathed the old beast to him last year, a heartfelt, if impractical, gift. Keaton had learned how to drive on the Bel Air, an athletic exercise in strength and hand-eye coordination. He'd taken a renewed interest in the car a few years ago when Rodger had installed new rings on the pistons and replaced the seals and gaskets, extending the life of the antique. Rodger had shown him how to adjust the timing, the function and parts of the distributor and carburetor, mechanical systems nowadays replaced by computers and fuel injection.

Keaton wiped the grease from under his nails. The old Chevy took a lot more care than a modern vehicle, but there was nothing else like it on the roads these days. He'd checked the points, a method for regulating electricity to the spark plugs, and the oil, brake fluid, and radiator. There were no sensors, no computer monitors, no power steering, no power brakes. And no air conditioning. Basic transportation with an extra dose of chrome.

Sixteen miles to the gallon, ready to hit the highway.

He and his friend Harry were going to take the car across country to a place just south of El Paso, an auto shop that specialized in Chevrolets. The Bel Air needed only minor body work, some new upholstering, and a fresh coat of paint. After that, it could be worth several times its current value. After searching the internet, sending photos, and speaking with several shops, the El Paso outfit seemed the most reputable and also offered Keaton the most money for it: $8,000.

Once he sold the car, he had something specific in mind for the cash.

He'd long considered starting a furniture repair shop, even while he'd patrolled the streets of Kabul in his final months in the army. He'd married right out of the service then divorced three years later, and although he'd had a couple of live-in girlfriends, he'd never remarried. He enjoyed some martial arts training and jobs where he worked mostly with his hands: landscaping, construction, engine repair. The years had taken their fair toll, complete with back strains and bursitis pains, but on the inside, he still felt like a tough young man, disciplined and forward-looking. He still stretched and worked with weights several times a week.

One of his favorite shops had been a historic blacksmith barn refurbished with jig saws and table saws, stacks of panels and boards, scraps of oak, cedar, and maple being re-shaped into something old and new at the same time. He could smell the raw sawdust, stains, and glue, feel the curve of hand-carved antique desks and tables and chairs. Woodworking was a way to satisfy his own brand of perfectionism, restoring form and order to craftmanship in need of repair.

And it seemed prudent to exchange his uncle's old Chevy for something more sensible, something with which he could earn some income.

Thank you, Uncle Rodger.

"Daydreaming again?"

Harry's voice startled him.

"Can I put my stuff in the trunk?"

"Oh, sure – it's open." Keaton pointed. He'd been close friends with Harry's older brother Leo, an army fire control specialist who'd lost his life to an improvised explosive device in Afghanistan. Keaton and Leo had been together in many of the same classes in high school, two misfits bound together for survival. Two weeks after graduation, they'd enlisted together.

To this day, memories of Leo tightened his chest.

Harry had been a sophomore when Keaton and Leo were seniors. Keaton and Harry had become friendly, too, before Leo died. After that, Keaton and Harry had drifted apart, but shared memories of Leo kept them circling back to each other. Harry was more of a free spirit than Leo had been, more philosophical about life, less reliable on task. But he reminded Keaton of Leo, too; the way he joked with people, the rumble of his voice, the angle of his jaw. When Keaton said he was looking for someone to help him drive across country to west Texas, Harry had volunteered.

He watched Harry walk to the car and lift the lid of the cavernous trunk. An oil-stained box full of tools and spare parts had been shoved into the left corner. Keaton had laid a single piece of luggage on the far-right side. A daypack, tent, blankets, and two sleeping bags lay next to the suitcase. A light brown tarp, trimmed and fitted to protect large sedans, was rolled next to the tent.

"Hey, do you mind if you drive first – take the first leg of the trip?" Harry asked.

"Fine by me."

"Did you put that cooler of food together?"

Keaton raised a finger. "Not yet." He turned and went back into his apartment.

******

Harry went to his own car, a rusted GM hatch-back, and lifted one of the green dry bags from the back. He tucked it behind the box of parts in the trunk of the Chevy then placed the second one on top of the first. He took a duffle bag with his clothes and gear for the trip, laid it in front of the parts box, loosened a blanket to cover the green bags, and closed the trunk.

CHAPTER 5

Lila sprinted away from the edge of the greenhouse and across an expanse of uncut grass. When she reached the trees where the woods began, she hurried to a spot where she could penetrate the tangled wall of brush and branches. She turned her shoulders right, then left, slipping between the saplings, stepping over fallen trunks and rocks, until she was several feet inside the living mesh. She bent at the knees and caught her breath. She turned behind her and stared at the field she'd just crossed, the rear corner of the greenhouse, and the farmhouse beyond.

Where Dr. Blackstone's body lay.

She could hardly believe he was dead.

The field was empty. Where was Wayland Jones, the USDA agent? Had he also escaped? Was he in trouble, too?

She squatted to the ground and waited, unsure what to do next. Moments stretched into minutes, and she wondered whether to return to the greenhouse or try to push her way deeper into the woods. Would her cell phone work here? Had the killer followed her? Would he hear her voice if she dialed 911?

Movement in her periphery sent a jolt up her spine. An irregular rustling disturbed the leaves, but the undergrowth was too tight for a clear view.

The sound stopped. Slowly, she leaned closer to the ground, hoping to make it harder for anyone to see her.

Pop! Pop!

A pistol fired over her head, close by, nearly upon her. She turned deeper into the woods and shuffled on her hands and feet, over the rocks. Low hung branches grabbed at her hair, yanking then releasing her, clinging to her shirt then slipping away. Her pack snagged against a maple tree, jarring her to a stop. She twisted out of the straps and untangled them.

She began again, clearing the maple and rising to her feet. She reshouldered her pack and searched for a trail. Ahead stretched a labyrinth of tangled brush and trees, the frantic strokes of a troubled painter. She pushed forward, ducking and turning into any small break she could find, spinning around tree trunks, shoving leaves and thorns to her side as she went.

She stopped behind the trunk of another maple tree, a spot where the jungle opened just a breath. A whisper of wind lifted scraps of leaves from the ground, whirling them upward, gliding them away. She heard the snap of a twig, brittle to her ear.

The shooter was following her.

She searched the canopy above, but the sky was hidden by the old growth trees and her sense of direction became muddled. She moved away from the sounds of the person behind her, walking steadily now, stepping methodically in as straight a line as she could imagine.

She came across a small game trail unexpectedly and turned onto it. She lengthened her stride, splitting the brush on either side of the narrow path until she broke into a run, heart thumping, crashing through.

The trail opened suddenly onto a grassy slope and all at once she'd stepped onto another planet, transported back to civilization. A wide line of macadam curved just ahead beyond the slope – an on-ramp for the freeway beyond. She needed to get out of the woods to find help.

She ran across the wide clearing, over the curb, and onto the shoulder on the other side and turned to get her bearings. No one had left the woods yet but at any moment the shooter could emerge and would not have to catch her – he could fire his gun across the empty field. To her right, the highway was maybe fifty yards up the road. To her left and farther away, the pavement led back into the streets of town.

Only the woods offered a place to hide, and she'd just run away from them.

A lone figure emerged at the edge of the tree line, a silhouette dark among the shadows, but unmistakably human.

She glanced toward the highway, then back down the ramp, then back at the gunman in the woods. She had to do something and had to do it now.

A large car growled its way up the ramp, rounding the corner, coming straight toward her. The thing was streaked with chrome and curves like she'd never seen before and it rolled heavily forward like a slow-motion movie of her own life, the shooter across the green, her own feet on the open grass, unable to move.

CHAPTER 6

Keith Wormwood stared at the row of binders on his bookshelf then glanced at the decanter of whiskey on his desk, desire swimming through his pale eyes. Fifty-two years old and thirty pounds overweight, he avoided exercise like it was a toothache and hung onto his marriage with the desperation of a drowning sailor.

Bars of light cast a grid across the plaster wall, sunlight slashing through cheap, plastic blinds. The room felt like a spectral prison; bars as real as metal overlaid his desk like in a Salvador Dali painting.

He went to the window and closed the blinds, softening the glare.

Stan Barber tapped the door to Wormwood's office, entering without ceremony. His business partner for nearly sixteen years. Barber's hair had thinned to a shiny pate, his face now anchored to thick lenses on heavy black frames. He carried a file under his arm and sat across from Wormwood's desk.

"Well?" Wormwood returned to his chair, rocking almost imperceptibly.

"That's not how I'd describe the quarterly report." Barber slapped it onto the desk.

Wormwood grunted. He'd already seen a draft of the latest profit and loss statement for Dragontree Agri-Economics, the troubled brainchild of Wormwood and Barber. Located in a rental district outside of Indianapolis, Dragontree invested heavily in genetic modification research in plants, including corn, soybeans, rice, and tomatoes. Few people realized how much of modern agriculture was the result of gene manipulation, from old-style plant selection by growers to a host of laboratory genetic engineering techniques – biolistics, electroporation, microinjection, agrobacterium. The future of agriculture lies in genetic manipulation and the biggest win, the hottest lottery ticket, lies in patent-protected licensing and distribution. Even the mere possession of plants with improved yield or drought resistance could be worth multiple millions of dollars in profit. Enough even for a little company like Dragontree to suddenly dominate the economic landscape.

Barber stared upward, beseeching the textured ceiling for divine intervention.

Wormwood had had the trappings of success – a cream and chrome Cadillac, a cherry-red Porsche, a townhouse in Belize. But the company had had no new patents in nearly eight years. Wormwood had sold his townhouse, traded in the Porsche, and watched his net worth shrink like leaves in the sun.

Barber had lost his twin engine Comanche to creditors and his wife to a cement contractor out of Brownsburg.

"We've got to get more creative to survive." Wormwood pushed the report back toward his partner, unwilling to own it.

Barber levelled his gaze. "We still have decent cash reserves in the bank, but if something doesn't break our way soon, our beloved company is going to go belly up."

"Damn it, Stan, that's not going to happen." Wormwood set his fists on the desk.

Barber opened his arms as if to say: how the hell can we avoid it?

"I've got a lead on a new development that could be substantial, the one that puts us in black ink again."

"Do I want to hear about yet another project that's supposed to save us?" Barber's tone made it clear that he did not. "I'm not getting involved in anything underhanded, you know." He delivered his next words like a dealer counting each card: "We've had that conversation."

Yes, they had. Wormwood released a heavy sigh.

Competition from the major biotech companies was tough on the little guys. Like so many things, winning the race depended on obtaining key information before your opponents did. You had to be creative to survive.

The big companies called it economic espionage, but Wormwood called it levelling the playing field. He had several inside contacts, people connected to genetic research projects who he'd paid in exchange for data and updates. Some he'd paid openly, on contract. Others had to be paid under the table.

All of them were prowling for the next opportunity.

His partner wanted the unattainable: results without risk, success without an aftertaste. Wormwood had tired of the game, but he and Barber had been through a lot in eighteen years, and he still felt a tug of loyalty. And Barber was a financial whiz – his investments in the stock market had kept Dragontree afloat for the last two years. Wormwood could hardly jettison the man.

"It's just research and development," Wormwood continued, tapping a finger on his desk. "My bailiwick."

"We have three more months. Then, we'd best be meeting with a bankruptcy attorney."

Wormwood winced as if some sharp-clawed cat had just tried to maul its way out of his chest.

Barber stood and straightened his glasses.

Neither man looked at the other. Barber waited until what could pass as polite silence filled the space between them and then left the room, closing the door behind him.

Wormwood sighed again and stared out the banded window. He'd mined his sources the day before yesterday and a promising tidbit had, in fact, emerged. Most promising, even. He allowed himself a quick grin, a pin-prick of hope, and reached for the whiskey.

He'd already put his associates in gear.

CHAPTER 7

Lila put one foot into the road and waved her arms at the speeding car, a plea for help, a quick ride out of danger.

"C'mon, c'mon, c'mon," she hissed, desperation in her voice. She stuck her thumb in the air and flexed at the knees, ready to run again. The faces of two older men grew larger as the blue sedan rumbled up the ramp. They looked up at her at the same time, eyes reaching hers. The passenger turned to the driver, and she could see the driver's lips moving, but the big car kept coming, no slowing, no hesitation, and she thought, oh shit, it was hopeless.

If they passed, she would be all alone again and completely in the open.

She glanced across the road at the tree line. He must still be there, the gunman, Dr. Blackstone's killer, but she could no longer tell where he was. She sensed that he'd backed into the shadows, waiting for traffic to flow past.

Suddenly, the sound of the engine dropped an octave and the car slowed quickly to a gentle roll. She ran to the window, which the passenger had already lowered.

"Need a lift?" the man asked, his smile wide and friendly.

The car came to a complete stop.

"Yes! Thank you, so much!" She moved to the back door, not waiting for another invitation, and tugged it open. She slipped the pack off her back, jumped onto the seat, and pulled the heavy door closed behind her.

"There's a seat belt," the passenger turned toward her and pointed.

She felt the car move forward, gaining speed. She set her pack on the floor by her feet, fastened the lap belt around her waist, and tried to take a deep breath. Her lungs hurt, her muscles ached, and her hands twitched like a smoker without a fix. She looked behind them and strained to see the shooter, but saw only brush and treetops and shaded grass. They drove steadily faster up the ramp, twisting her view of the woods, and soon she could see only the concrete road behind them as they merged onto the open freeway.

Oh my god. She turned forward in her seat and let her shoulders drop. Then she noticed the front passenger watching her, a hint of concern crossing his dark blue eyes.

She cleared her throat. "Thanks for picking me up." The simple declaration, the sound of her own voice, seemed otherworldly. She clasped her hands together. "It's been a bad morning and I really needed the ride."

"No worries." He smiled a row of pearly teeth and his eyes crinkled like some secret in life amused him. He wore his white hair in a ponytail, a progressive who'd forgotten which century he was in. "I'm Harry, by the way, and this is Keaton." He pointed at the driver, who kept his eyes on the road and nodded.

"I'm Lila."

"Where you headed?"

"West," she sighed, glancing at the freeway sign for I-70. Where did she want them to drop her off? Where did she need to go? Who could she call for help?

"Us, too. All the way to El Paso, in fact."

"Oh…" she thought for a moment. "Well, I'm not going that far, but…" she tried to think quickly. "How about St. Louis?"

"Sure. Be there by the end of the day."

St. Louis? Well, it was the first name that came to mind. Why not Terre Haute? Who knows why things pop into your brain when you're running from a killer? And that's fine. It would put plenty of distance between her and the shooter and she could contact the police there, get some protection, tell them what had happened. Yes, that was as good a plan as any. If she could calm her nerves a bit.

"Hey, uh, are you OK?" Harry nodded toward her left arm.

She glanced at a deep scratch where blood had smeared across her skin. "Oh, yeah, sure. I ran through some thorns."

"Here…" he handed her a paper towel. "There's water in the cooler on the floor. Get yourself something to drink and you can clean up with this."

"Thanks." She pulled a bottle of water from the small cooler, dabbed it on the towel, and wiped her arm.

"Trash bag is somewhere back there, by your feet."

"Yes, got it."

"Hey, you know, if you'd like, we could drop you at a shelter there in St. Louis. We can find an address…" He and Keaton shared a glance then Harry held his cell phone in the air, showing her that he could search for a domestic violence program.

"Oh, no, that's…"

"It's all right. Maybe your boyfriend's an ass. You need to talk to someone about this." Harry shifted in his seat, facing her more directly.

"No, it's not that…" Blackstone's sightless eyes filled her mind again. She saw herself shaking him, the man still right there with her, just asleep but gone, too; never to speak again. She pretended to examine her arm, afraid to look at Harry for fear her anguish would flood her away.

"Whatever you like, just let us know." Harry turned forward again. "We're glad to help you out."

"Hey, Harry, I'm going to pull off at the next exit and get some gas," Keaton pointed at a highway sign.

"About eight miles ahead."

"Already?"

"Forgot to top off the tank. And this hunk of metal doesn't exactly break records for gas mileage."

"Well, not the good kind of records."

She sat back against the seat, relaxing her shoulders, trying to focus on her surroundings. Harry's hair was long, but Keaton's was trimmed tightly against his head. Instead of bucket seats, the front was one long bench, wide enough for another person to sit between Harry and Keaton. The speedometer was a clock-like dial housed inside a rounded tubing, a giant eyepiece on a telescope. Two smaller displays were mounted on either side of the speedometer like instruments on a glitzy aircraft. The dash was all metal, no cushions, no padding, curving forward to a flat area above the glove box. Chrome letters with a line connecting them announced the vehicle as a "Chevrolet." Small window wings were angled near the front windshield.

She felt a sideways tug as Keaton turned them down an off-ramp and to an intersection below. He rolled to a stop and turned left on a two-lane road that ducked under the highway. They drove about a quarter mile farther and down a gentle slope toward a gas station on the right.

"Hey, Harry. No big deal…" Keaton nodded toward the rearview mirror, "…but that brown Nissan back there seems to be tagging us."

CHAPTER 8

Someone was following them? Lila's stomach dropped.

Keaton braked at one of the pumps.

"Probably just want to admire the old Chevy. Or try to buy it from you." Harry opened his door and slid outside.

Lila glanced behind but saw no other vehicle.

"Want something from the store?" Harry offered.

"No. No, thank you." She turned in her seat, searching the road behind them, when she found a Nissan parked on the side of the road. Why would someone be following them? Could it be the shooter from Blackstone's greenhouse? How could he have caught up with them? Did the shooter have someone helping him?

She took a quick drink from the water bottle and watched as Keaton walked to the back of the car. A steady ding, ding, ding marked the passage of gasoline from the pump into the fuel tank. Harry wetted the front windshield with a squeegee and wiped it clean.

She laced her fingers together and held them tight.

Soon, Keaton and Harry were done and back in the car, Keaton behind the wheel again.

"All set?" Keaton asked.

She stared at the parked brown car and pressed her hands until her knuckles turned white.

Harry followed her line of sight. "You know that car?"

"No," she said quickly. "Well…"

"Really? Is that guy following you?"

She felt Harry's gaze and turned to look to him. "I should get out here, guys. No need to bring you into this, in case he really is following me."

"Hey, let's not get too impulsive here," Keaton said, watching her in the rearview mirror. "I get this kind of attention sometimes. It's just someone admiring the old classic." He patted the front dash. "An antique, really."

"Well…"

"I'll show you," Keaton said. "I'll turn right when we go out of here, away from the highway. He'll lose interest and go back to the highway and then we can turn around."

"He's right." Harry nodded at her and turned to Keaton. "Yeah, let's do that" He pointed the way.

They were moving again before she could think it through, turning out of the gas station and onto a narrow country road that ran through a thick tangle of woods.

She watched the pavement ahead for a moment then took a cautious look behind them.

The brown car was speeding toward them now, boldly chasing their bumper, coming closer.

"Well, shit," Harry announced.

"What!" Keaton glared at the mirror.

"You ass…" Harry said to the Nissan behind them. He turned toward Keaton. "Get going."

Keaton jiggled the gas pedal, pulling them faster.

The brown car held its distance.

The old road curved sharply to the right. Keaton accelerated through the turn, veering over the center line, and the car behind them lost some ground. The road dipped sharply down hill and Keaton let their momentum build. Trees hung tightly to the shoulder, branches hanging above them in a blur, the Chevy tossing them up, down, then bouncing on old springs and shocks, careening onto level pavement and into another turn.

Lila held her right hand tightly against the back of the front seat, her left shoulder angled into the rear. The car behind had disappeared beyond the curve. Keaton sped across open ground, the woods retreating behind them. They climbed quickly up another hill, this one steeper and longer than the last. The crest came quickly, and the old Bel Air lifted on its suspension for a moment, flying, it seemed, into another turn and onto another straightaway. A dirt road entered the highway on their left, then another on their right.

"Keaton!" Harry pointed toward a third dirt road a half mile ahead on their right.

"Got it."

She braced herself and the Chevy lurched downward on its front wheels, brakes squealing, shoving her into the seat in front of her. The tires screeched for a moment, pulling them into the center of the empty road. Keaton's chest pressed against the steering wheel, his fingers underneath it and, as they slowed, he spun the wheel clockwise, pulling hand over hand against the weight of it. The car leaned into the turn, lifting Lila from the seat. They passed the dirt road by a few feet and Keaton kept turning until they'd backtracked onto the packed ground. He pushed the gas down again, momentum pulling her back into the seat again and they bounced across the rutted earth. A hundred yards down, the road turned sharply left and to an open field. Keaton spun the wheel again, jarring across the tall grass until they'd turned back, pointed toward the dirt road.

Keaton brought the Chevy to a full stop in the weeds. Dust swirled past their windows and out into the open air. She couldn't see the highway from here.

They sat there, the engine rumbling, their hearts thumping.

Surely, the brown car would have seen them turn off the highway and soon would block them in.

But they waited, all eyes on the path ahead.

One minute passed. Then another.

"I'm going to check," Harry said, sliding out the front door. "Stay put."

He trotted to the edge of the trees, ponytail bobbing as he went.

Then he disappeared around the corner.

Lila let loose a low moan. What the hell was happening?

Three more minutes passed.

Keaton glanced at her. "I'm going to check on him."

"No – wait," she pointed. "He's here."

Harry ran to the car and climbed inside. "All clear. They had to have gone past. I don't see any sign of them."

"We'll turn back to the highway," Keaton nodded.

"I'll walk ahead of you and signal you if it's still clear. Follow me but stay back as far as you can." Harry slid from the car again and went quickly down the road.

Keaton eased slowly across the field and onto the dirt tracks. After they passed the bend, Lila could see Harry jogging to the highway. He stopped and peered around the trees, waving them to follow his lead.

Keaton drove more quickly now and skidded to a stop forty feet from the pavement. Harry ran back and climbed into the car.

"All clear."

Their tires spun dirt into the air and they reached the pavement in a jarring bounce. Keaton wrenched the wheel to the left and they accelerated down the highway, past a bend in the road, and down the hill they'd come up earlier, gaining speed to the bottom, the Chevy weighing down on its suspension again, then recoiling upward and levelling out. She stared out the back window, praying, willing the road to remain empty and they passed another bend in the road, barreling back toward the gas station and Interstate 70.

CHAPTER 9

The air crackled with static electricity and the faint scent of sweaty socks. Keaton opened the breeze wing, the triangular piece of glass near the front windshield, and a gust of wind scattered the tension like snowflakes in a storm.

"That was a bit of a rush." Keaton glanced toward Lila and drove onto the ramp for I-70.

"Hell, that was some wild-ass driving back there, especially in this big tank." Harry patted the dash.

They passed an overhead sign for Terre Haute.

Harry twisted back to see Lila. "You recognize that car? Is that guy following you?"

"No. I don't recognize him or the car." She looked to the floor. Why would someone follow them so aggressively, like that? It must be connected to Dr. Blackstone's killing…

"Well, whoever he is, he's way behind us now."

Keaton adjusted the wing.

"But if he was following us, he'd figure we would get back on I-70, eventually." Harry pointed ahead of them. "Wouldn't he?"

"But he couldn't possibly catch up with us now." Lila looked at Harry, hope bubbling to the surface.

"We're not exactly speeding in this old tank." Harry rubbed his chin. "The Bel Air wasn't a high-performance car in 1960 and it sure as hell can't beat a modern, fuel-injected, engine."

"We can stay at the speed limit," Keaton offered. "But if that guy is determined to catch us, he could go 80 or 85…"

"A car driving 85 miles per hour would be 10 miles an hour faster than us." Harry's eyes narrowed, a glimpse of concern, but then he seemed to stop himself. He watched her for a moment and his brow relaxed with a hint of mischief. "So, if one car is 15 miles ahead of a second car, and the second car is going 10 miles an hour faster, let's see…" He lifted his gaze to the roof of the car, a nascent grin on his lips. "Accounting for the uncertainty principle and the rotation of the Earth…applying the mass-ratio algorithm…carry the nine…" he counted silently on his fingers.

"Ha!" Keaton glanced at Lila in the rearview mirror. "A hundred bucks if you help me throw this joker out of the car." He grinned.

"Fascist," Harry teased.

"Two hundred bucks if the car's still moving," Keaton said.

Lila smiled.

"We have 30 to 60 minutes." Harry folded his arms, a look of mock satisfaction on his face.

"Ever helpful," Keaton said.

"So, it's anybody's guess?" she asked. "But how could they find us in all this traffic?"

"We're in a 1960 royal blue Chevy Bel Air classic." Keaton kept his eyes on the highway.

"We're like a curse in the middle of communion," Harry added.

"Yeah, I got that." She'd sounded more harshly than she'd intended.

Keaton shifted in his seat. "How about we find a quiet place to pull off for a while?"

"There's a state park just over the border, into Illinois." Harry consulted a map folded on his lap.

"We could take the back roads for a while…" Keaton offered.

Lila straightened her shirt. "Yeah, I could sure use a break about now."

CHAPTER 10

They drove without further conversation for some time, staying on I-70 into Illinois and on to Clarksville. Lila watched behind them the entire way, and when they curved away from the freeway, no one followed them. She felt her chest relax as they headed south on state route one, a straight, two-way highway into the countryside. She finally turned forward again, resting her back against the seat.

"There's a gas station up there, Keaton, with picnic tables and space off to the side." Harry pointed.

"Good spot."

Lila nodded.

They pulled under the station canopy and Keaton topped off the gas tank. He moved the car into some shade by a pair of tables and parked. Lila looked around and slid out of the seat into the cool autumn air.

A blue pickup truck drove past the station, but

otherwise the road was empty. A thicket of poplar trees, Populus tremula, waved lemon-lime leaves at each other, a kind of pre-winter farewell. She hefted her pack to her shoulders and walked to the nearest picnic table, stretching her legs and back.

Harry sat on the other side of the table and pushed a can of diet root beer toward her.

"Thank you! You don't have to…"

Harry shooed her words away.

Keaton sat next to Harry, opened his drink, and took a gulp. It was the first chance she'd had to take a good look at the two men.

Harry's eyes were tightened with concern, blue irises shining as if the source of light was behind them, glowing inside his skull. His face roughly matched his frame – long and lanky, sun-worn skin hanging like a loose shirt drying on a line. His hair was white and long, still pulled into a ponytail, and she found herself wondering how old he was. He could be fifty, or seventy, and she'd not know the difference. He reminded her of one of her professors, a man of political moxie with the passion of the civil rights movement.

Keaton folded his hands in front of him, muscled forearms resting on the table-top. His hair was gray, cropped so short the color was hard to notice until you were close to him. A trim, charcoal beard covered his face and neck and his eyes seemed to absorb the sunlight like a pair of black holes. Stocky and slightly shorter than average, she thought he must be an old wrestler or maybe a boxer, retired but still in shape. A tough old guy.

Strangers to her. But here they were, willing to rescue her from an abuser. Or a killer.

"Well," she cleared her throat. "I'm grateful for you guys stopping to pick me up, and I'm so, so sorry about that weird car chase…"

"No harm, no foul," Harry said.

"Still…" she wrapped her fingers around the can.

"We'll still get you to a battered woman's shelter," Harry checked with Keaton, who nodded in agreement, "if that's what you want."

"That's right," Keaton nodded. "We'll take you right there, if you like."

Lila owed them an explanation, that much she knew, and then she'd form a plan to move on without bothering them anymore.

She cleared her throat. "I'm not running from an abusive boyfriend or anything like that. Let me start at the beginning…" She explained that she was a student seeking a degree in botany, that she'd found a great summer job with Dr. Blackstone and the kinds of things they were studying, and that she'd come to work early this morning – well, she'd tried to be early – got her coffee at the office and found seeds to mail for the doctor. "I walked outside, to go to the greenhouse, and there he was – Dr. Blackstone – dead in the grass. And the blood…"

She stared at her fingers.

"Shit!" Harry clenched his hands into fists.

"No…" Keaton straightened his back.

She nodded, wiping her eyes with her sleeve.

"What the hell?" Harry asked.

She looked at Harry, then at Keaton. "Yeah" she repeated. "What the hell."

"What did you do?" Keaton asked.

"I ran back inside and ran into Mr. Jones, the agriculture guy…"

"Who?"

"Wayland Jones. He works for the Department of Agriculture. He was there to see what Dr. Blackstone had to present. I'm pretty sure the doctor was going to tell us something really important, but he never got the chance…"

"And…?" Harry prompted.

"Jones said he'd called 911 but that somebody was still in the building. So, I grabbed my pack and ran outside, out past Dr. Blackstone's…body…and past the greenhouse, into the woods."

Keaton leaned forward. "Into the woods?"

"Yeah. I looked back and couldn't see Mr. Jones. I have no idea whether he's okay or not, but then I heard someone in the bushes, and they chased me – even shot at me – and I came to the edge of the trees and onto a lawn-like area, near the on-ramp for the highway. I ran across the road and turned back to look and could see someone at the edge of the trees, and that's when I heard your car, and you came up the ramp and I held out my thumb and you stopped for me." She took a deep breath.

The men stared at her.

"Thank God you stopped for me! I owe you guys my life!" She bit her lip, her eyes held wide.

"I almost didn't..." Keaton said to Harry.

They sat in silence for what felt like an eternity, quiet draping over them until the stillness begged for the sound of a human voice, any kind of communication at all, and she broke the spell.

"That's why I need you guys to take off – keep going on your trip and leave me here. I can call for help from the gas station, figure out what to do next."

Harry and Keaton spoke over each other.

"Not so fast..."

"Like bloody hell you will..."

CHAPTER 11

"Is there family we can call for you? Or take you to?" Keaton slid his hand across his head.

"Not really…"

"No one?" he asked.

Her mother had died four years ago. The moment Lila received the news was chiseled into her memory: the doctor's pale scrubs, the hard plastic seat, ammonia laced with lemon as if a load of citrus would gladden the reek of a morgue. Her mother had been crushed by a tractor trailer that had skidded across an icy bridge, hard into her two-door Subaru and the concrete abutment. The winter storm had killed eight other people that day, one of the worst pileups in Toronto's history, but that was no solace for any of the survivors. Two years later, her father married a woman so unlike her mother that Lila wondered why her parents had ever gotten together in the first place. An only child, Lila had become virtually and then literally emancipated, a stray freshman hiding in the vaults of student housing, burying herself in her studies.

Her grandpa in Michigan had died of heart failure a year before that. Her grandma had passed away seven months after her grandpa.

She tried to clear her head.

"Boyfriend?"

"Not currently."

"Hard to believe." Harry smiled, a weak attempt to cheer her up.

"We'll get you to the police, then." Keaton tapped a finger on the picnic table, a flesh and bone exclamation point.

"Good god, that's not how to help her, man." Harry's eyes swelled into marbles.

"Of course that's what we need to do," Keaton said.

"You never, ever, trust the cops, Keaton, we've been through this before..."

"This is not one of your cheap spy novels, Harry. We've got a murder on our hands!"

"That's exactly why it's dangerous."

"Not from the cops, it's not."

"How do we know the feds aren't involved? Genetic research, national security..."

The point struck her as a bit extreme. Then she remembered her violation of the visa, her plan to visit the USCIS tomorrow. And that Dr. Blackstone was no longer alive to run interference for her.

Keaton looked to the sky, exasperation on his face. "So, who's going to help us with this?"

"We don't run blindly to the authorities is all I'm saying." Harry folded his arms.

"Hey, uh…" Lila began.

"What?" Harry and Keaton spoke the same word together, deflecting their annoyance toward her.

"Sorry," Keaton mumbled.

"Hey, I'm saying that you don't have to worry about it at all." She tucked a strand of hair behind her ears.

Harry stood and walked away from the table.

"It's a little complicated, from where he sees it," Keaton whispered.

"Why?" Lila leaned forward.

"Well, he's never trusted authority. Tiptoes around it whenever he can," Keaton shrugged. "It's just straight up paranoia. It's how he is…"

But she quickly understood Harry's point of view. If she went to USCIS now and reported her violation of the visa, would they simply forgive it? In light of Dr. Blackstone's murder? A sharp edge of guilt sliced through her – how could she think about herself after the poor doctor had been shot dead? She rubbed her eyes for a moment, trying to focus on her surroundings.

A gust of wind shuddered the leaves, the sound like a dozen tiny maracas.

She liked these two old guys; friends traveling across the country in an antique tank of a car, willing to change course for a random hitchhiker, willing to help someone in need. They weren't exactly race car drivers or Navy SEALs or Secret Service, but they seemed smart and skilled and smelled a little like her grandpa. She trusted them.

"You should do what you want to, of course." Keaton laid his palms on the table. "We're also willing to help if you want us to. Maybe we help a lot, maybe a little… it's up to you."

"I'd be grateful. Hell, I already am," she choked on her words a bit.

"Then let's find a way forward." Keaton's beard expanded with his smile. "Just…"

"Yes?"

"Don't tell that old hippie what I said about him, OK?" He winked at her.

"Of course not." She smiled.

"That fed you mentioned…he's not FBI, is he?"

"No. Department of Agriculture."

Keaton nodded. "I have an idea…" He whispered in her ear.

She nodded. "Got it."

CHAPTER 12

Wormwood twirled in his office chair, sliding papers onto the floor in a manic spin. Two days ago, he'd finally caught a live one – a lead on genetically modified seeds with enormous potential. At first, the significance did not dawn on him. But when his source explained it, he'd nearly burst a blood vessel.

His advantage was that he had this knowledge early. His problem was that the modification technique had an element of randomness – the developer had used low-level radiation and then tested the plants over many years. Replicating the result directly could take many years as well. What he really needed were the seeds themselves, which he could examine and replicate and use to obtain a patent.

He'd negotiated a payment to his source, so long as the information was accurate and updated on a daily basis. They'd not yet settled on a price if the seeds turned out to be as real as they seemed, but he'd decided on an offer – five percent of gross return for five years minus costs for distribution. In fact, he knew he'd go as high as fifteen percent, if he had to. Generous, yes, but either arrangement would save Dragontree Agri-Economics, probably his marriage, and install him as the new corporate king of the genetic engineering world.

After what his men had called a "thorough search," they'd concluded that the seeds must have been taken by a young woman who worked on the project and who'd run away from the greenhouse with a daypack. At least, that was their excuse for failing to find the special berries. There were rows and rows of shrubs and the greenhouse was now a crime scene, so finding the mother plant was highly impractical. So, it seemed that the problem had turned into a cross-country race, a task far too important to entrust only to those skip-tracers – bail bondsmen who muscled their way through life. Sure, he'd put them on the trail, too, but they'd already missed at least one important opportunity.

It was time to up the ante.

He lifted the phone and dialed a private contractor he'd used once before with some success. The secretary transferred his call.

"Mr. Wormwood?" asked the voice on the other end of the line. "How can we help you today?"

"Phillip, yeah, it's me. I need a rush job and I'm ready to pay your usual fee plus a five percent bonus for quick results."

"Ten is the motivation my guys are accustomed to."

Wormwood rolled his eyes. "Then ten it is."

"What do you have?"

"I need to find two men and a young woman going cross country, heading west."

"Names?"

"Just the girl's and the general direction, but we learned they're driving a 1960 Chevy with Indiana license plates."

"Oh. Yeah, that's enough to get started."

"We need to intercept them, so I need to know who they are, who their friends are, who they might stay with as they travel."

"So, these folks are all travelling together?"

"We don't actually know. It seems like the girl may have just hitched a ride with them," Wormwood said.

"So, it's possible she's not even with them anymore?"

"Yeah, unfortunately."

"Got it. Let me start with what you have on the girl, and I can find the owners of the car and research them. By chance, are any of them ex-military? We've got some contacts through there…"

"I don't know." Wormwood gave Phillip the details he had.

"Anything else?"

"I've got two men on it already. I want you to coordinate with them, but Phil, they're not really up for the job. You're in charge."

"On it."

"Call me soon."

CHAPTER 13

"Come here," Keaton waved at Harry. "We think we've got a compromise."

Harry lumbered toward them, arms swinging, and sat at the picnic table again.

"Well," Lila began, "I sort of know this guy from the Department of Agriculture, Wayland Jones. He's the one who called 911 and warned me that the shooter was still there, at the farmhouse. He may have saved my life. He's a fed, but he already knows a little bit about what Dr. Blackstone has been working on. Maybe he knows more about it than I do, since we have this federal funding grant…"

Harry glanced at Keaton.

"Anyway, I have Jones's phone number. I can call him and see if he's OK and see what happened after I left. And let him know I'm OK."

Keaton reached into a small cooler he'd brought

from the car. He laid out three sandwiches wrapped in foil and a roll of paper towels on the table. "It's not like she'll be talking to the FBI or something. She won't turn herself in, so to speak. She'll stay with us. We won't tell this Jones guy where we are. We'll get information from him and keep travelling down the road and keep thinking about what to do next." He folded his fingers together.

Harry thought for a moment, glancing at Keaton, then Lila.

"It's Lila's idea." Keaton pointed at her.

"Of course, it is," Harry huffed. "A damn good one, too."

"See what we can achieve when you go for a walk in the woods?" Keaton waved his hand in the direction Harry had gone. A smirk rose on his lips, but he pulled it back, a façade of serious thought.

"What about the car that tried to follow us?" she asked.

"We'll keep going and keep a sharp eye." Harry nodded at her.

She glanced at the sandwich in front of her and tore into the wrapping. Harry and Keaton ate as well, the three of them lost in wordless rumination.

Nearly done, she patted her lips with a paper towel and rested her arms on the table.

Keaton swallowed. "Did you say you're studying botany at the university? What got you interested in that?"

She leaned forward, appreciating the opportunity

to talk about her studies – anything other than Dr. Blackstone's murder. "Because plants are absolutely amazing. You know, we came from a common ancestor. Six hundred million years ago, some plant decided to pull up its roots and walk around, and here we are."

Harry smiled at the thought.

"They're sensory creatures, like us. Leaves have rudimentary vision – lenses on the epidermis. And roots are a collective organism, like a colony of insects or a flock of birds, showing what are called 'swarm behavior patterns.' They're an integrated web of sensors, sharing information and reacting with a decentralized intelligence. And, of course, plants are the engine of life on Earth. We humans, and all the other animals, are completely dependent on them."

"Makes me want to start classes." Keaton nodded.

"And they have incredible medicinal properties." Harry lifted a finger in the air.

"Leave it to Harry to go straight to that…" Keaton tilted his eyes toward his friend.

They each chewed on another bite of sandwich.

"Well?" Harry looked at her, his question ambiguous.

But she knew what he was asking. "Yeah, I can't procrastinate forever." She pushed aside what was left of her sandwich. "Guess I'll make that call to Jones now."

"Do you mind keeping the phone on speaker? We'll be quiet," Harry said.

"Sure." She pulled the phone from her pocket, placed it next to her, and found Wayland Jones' phone number among her contacts. She glanced at Harry and Keaton and pressed "dial."

"Field agent Jones here."

Harry mouthed the question: "Agent?"

"Mr. Jones, this is Lila here…"

"Lila, my god, are you all right?" Jones' voice accelerated. "What happened after you left? Are you hurt? Where are you?"

"One question at a time," she pleaded.

"Hey, sorry, but tell me…"

"Of course. Well, I ran out of the farmhouse, across that small field and into the woods."

"I lost sight of you after you went behind the greenhouse."

She chewed her lower lip for a moment. "Somebody was behind me, chasing me. They fired a couple of shots, and I ran into the woods and a couple of guys picked me up and gave me a ride."

Harry spread his hands and whispered, "Ask him…"

"Oh, god, I'm just glad you're OK," Jones said. "Where are you now?"

"Yeah, I'm OK but what happened after I ran off? Did the police arrive? Was the killer still there? Did they chase you?"

"Seriously, Lila, where are you now?"

She glanced from Harry to Keaton. "Just off I-70,

at a rest stop."

"I'll come and get you."

Harry and Keaton shook their heads.

She asked again, "Did you see the killer? Did he chase you, too?"

"No, I never saw him. You went straight out of the building, and I went left, along the side of the farmhouse and around the corner, where I stayed until the sheriff arrived. I assume the sirens scared the killer off. He must have kept going, like you did, 'cause no one found him. No one knows who it might be or where he would have gone."

"How…how did he kill Dr. Blackstone?" she asked.

"Pistol shot in the back, Lila."

"Unbelievable."

"Yeah. Why would someone kill him? He was such a nice old guy."

"I have the same question. But he told me he was going to announce something important this morning. He must have said something to you, too?"

"Yeah, he called me last night and asked me to come by early." Jones cleared his throat. "He had some surprising test results, he said. He tried to explain it to me, but really, I'm not sure I got the gist of it right. Something about random low-level radiation experiments and oxygenation rates. I was looking forward to a full explanation, but I found him there, dead, the same as you did. I went inside to call 911 then heard someone come into the farmhouse, so I held back until I realized it was you. But then I heard someone else and figured that had to be the killer and, sure enough, he chased after you."

"Oh my god."

"Yeah. Tell me where you are, exactly, and I'll come pick you up. We can go to the sheriff together."

"I'm just still in shock, Mr. Jones…"

"…call me Wayland…"

"…and I need some time to process all this. I'll call you back, OK?"

"Lila – we don't know who killed Dr. Blackstone or why. Or whether he's after you, right now."

Keaton stared at her, his lips tight as a pencil line. Harry drew a finger across his throat, signaling her to end the conversation.

"I gotta go." She hung up and set the phone on the table. "Well, shit."

"That about says it all." Harry nodded.

CHAPTER 14

"Should I have Jones come pick me up?" she asked. Would he help her explain her predicament to the US-CIS? Or would he make it worse? What happened to the doctor was terrible, absolutely dreadful, but she had to consider her visa problem, too.

"Do you trust him?" Keaton asked.

"I don't know him," she replied. She had no reason to distrust him, but he hadn't earned her confidence, either. Then again, she was trusting Harry and Keaton and she hardly knew them. But maybe that was part of the reason why – they had absolutely no involvement with Dr. Blackstone or his work, so they couldn't be mixed up with his murder. They were helping her and, she had to admit, she kind of liked the old guys.

"Smart thinking. Always question authority." Harry nodded.

"Don't always do anything, except think things

through," Keaton admonished. "Sometimes authority enforces the rules for good reasons."

"Says the good soldier." Harry crossed his arms.

"Says the anarchist." Keaton's eyes narrowed but his lips rose in a grin.

"So," Harry turned his gaze toward Lila. "Just what the hell have you and your doctor been working on?"

"Genetics. Dr. Blackstone's been working for years on modifications to the genetic codes of mustard seeds, rice, chokecherries, some grasses…" She tucked the last of her sandwich into her cheeks.

"To what end?" Keaton asked.

"Let her swallow, will you?" Harry said.

"Well, it depends." She finished her bite. "Dr. Blackstone is – was – focused on creating gene mutations with low-level radiation treatments and second, third, or fourth generation plants, to see what resulted. Of course, higher yields were good, but caloric content, resistance to pesticides, oxygenation rates, CO_2 storage capacities." She waved her hand, indicating a long list of potential objectives.

"Would someone kill him over his studies?" Harry tossed a crumple of foil into the trash.

"God, no. I mean, I can't imagine…" She tugged at her ear lobe.

"But we should assume that he was the target." Harry stood and stretched his arms. "I mean, seeing as how he was the one who was shot."

They thought about that for a moment.

"Sorry. I didn't mean to sound flippant about it." Harry shuffled his feet in the dirt.

"You said he had some kind of announcement for you?" Keaton asked.

"Oh, that's true. He'd been pretty cheery lately. Energized. He hinted that he'd found something in his tests, and he said he'd explain them to me."

They sat in silence for a while. What the hell had Blackstone been working on?

She suddenly remembered the bag of seeds and leaves she was supposed to mail for the doctor.

"Wait here," she said to them. She went to the old car, retrieved her daypack, and came back to the table. She unzipped the main compartment and pulled out the clear baggie of seeds.

"What's that?" Harry leaned forward.

"Something Dr. Blackstone wanted me to mail." She pulled the handwritten note from the bag and read it aloud:

Mail to F. Knox, Box 1449, Fabens, TX

PVRI-mod.

IRGA indicates ± 374,000 kg/year/per adult plant

sequestration: ± 984% of Sweetgum - "magic beans"!

"Fort Knox?" Harry asked. "That's in Tennessee, not Texas."

"Why would he send something to Fort Knox?" Lila asked.

"It says 'F' Knox, not 'Fort Knox'," Keaton said.

"That must be a different place," Lila held the paper out for Keaton and Harry to see.

"Where is Fabens?" Harry asked.

"I think it's south of El Paso," Keaton said.

"So, what does 'PVRI-mod' mean?" Harry looked at Lila.

"It's a plant symbol, but off-hand I don't know which plant."

"IRGA?" Harry asked.

"IRGA stands for infra-red gas analyzer. It compares the CO_2 – carbon dioxide – passing into a chamber surrounding a leaf or plant and the CO_2 leaving the chamber. In other words, it allows you to figure out the amount of CO_2 that's absorbed by the leaves of a plant."

"Is that what this is? Here," Keaton pointed to the note: "± 374,000 kg/year/per adult plant sequestration."

"Right," she nodded. "The plus and minus sign means the number is an approximation."

"Is that number important?" Keaton asked.

"I'd have to check it, but it seems awfully high…"

"So, what's 'sweetgum'?" Harry asked.

"Must be the American sweetgum tree. But these seeds don't look like sweetgum…" Lila pulled the note back and looked at it again. "What does he mean by 'magic beans'?"

Harry glanced into the air. "There's a bean stalk somewhere?"

"Be serious," Keaton said.

"...or at least a boy named Jack," he grinned.

"I have no idea," Lila sighed. "But," she raised a finger. "If we can get to a computer or a public library, I can research 'PVRI' and what the sequestration is for sweetgum."

"I thought your generation had laptops attached to your hips," Keaton pointed toward her.

"I have a smartphone, but my battery's dead."

"The car has a cigarette lighter, to recharge it," Keaton said.

"But I don't have an adapter for that."

"All I have is a flip-top. A dumb phone," Harry said.

Keaton reached over and lifted the baggie onto the table. Plum colored orbs, nearly black and deeply wrinkled, rolled against each other, dried berries covering kernels the size of black peppers. Several darkened leaves, their edges curled and brittle, shifted among the seeds.

"What the hell are these?" Keaton asked.

They stared at the bag of seeds for several moments.

"Magic beans," Harry replied.

"Then we'd better not be waiting around for the giant to find us," Keaton said, nodding toward the Chevy.

CHAPTER 15

Keaton spread a map of the United States across the table and stared at it. "OK. Let's stay on the back roads and get to Effington, Illinois. It looks like a big enough place for a library or such, someplace you can get onto a computer." He looked up at Lila. "And recharge your phone. Then we can get back on the freeway if we want to."

She stared into the woods beyond the picnic area, wondering what her next steps should be; what Dr. Blackstone had discovered; whether there might be someone trying to find her; whether to admit her visa violation to the INS; whether to ask Harry and Keaton for even more assistance.

"Listen, Lila," Harry began. "Keaton's selling the old Chevy to a restoration place in El Paso, an auto shop that specializes in fixing up old Chevys and selling them to collectors. We're heading west. This F. Knox is in Fabens, Texas, south of El Paso. Instead of mailing those seeds to F. Knox, why not deliver them in person? Find out just what F. Knox is, and why Blackstone would ask you to get the seeds there."

She rubbed her hand across her forehead. "Re-ally? I mean, you guys would let me come with you all that way?"

"Of course. Hey, we're happy to help you out, and we want to know what F. Knox and these seeds are all about too, you know." Harry folded his arms across his chest.

"I don't have any fresh clothes, any sup-plies," she said.

"We'll find a thrift store in Effington. We've got road trip food enough for all."

"What about over night? Are you guys staying in hotels or such?"

Keaton rubbed his chin. "We have tents and sleep-ing bags and figured we'd either camp at some of those RV campsites or hit a hotel, either way."

"OK." Just knowing what she would be doing for the next few days was a bigger relief than she'd expected. "I really appreciate it."

Harry waved his hand dismissively.

They gathered themselves back into the car, Harry driving this time, and rode along a two-lane road through the countryside, heading west then northwest. Lila let herself relax on the back seat, sliding down below the windows and into a light nap. After a while, she noticed the car slowing and speeding up more frequently and peeked up to see what was happening.

"You slept," Keaton said.

"Yeah, I think so. Where are we?"

"Coming into Effington. Can your smartphone tell us where to find a library?"

"No battery, remember?"

"Oh, yeah." Keaton opened a map onto his lap and ran his finger down the page. "There's a map of the city here…and here's City Hall. I bet the library is nearby."

"Where do I go?" Harry asked.

"Left at the next light, then straight a few blocks."

They soon reached the center of town, a mixture of glass and metal storefronts among concrete government offices.

"Follow the sign," Lila pointed to a blue marker.

They turned again and pulled into a parking lot behind a courthouse. The library was a stout brick with automated sliding doors at the entrance and tinted windows facing the street. After using the restrooms, they found a bank of computers and Lila sat at the nearest one. She plugged her smartphone in to recharge the battery and began a search on the desktop computer for "F. Knox."

"Feels like home," Harry remarked to Keaton. They wandered about, perusing the texts on display, opening books, reading a bit, then moving on.

Lila expected "F. Knox" to be a location, maybe a factory or a courthouse or such, but instead the results were names of individuals – William, Steven, George. She added "botany" to the search and found a Frances Knox, Ph.D. biological scientist out of the University of South Dakota. Could this be the right person? She added "Dr. Blackstone" to the search. She discovered a research paper published by Knox and Blackstone in 1992 about low-level radiation treatments as random genetic modifiers among certain crops. They knew each other! Blackstone must have been sending the seeds to a trusted colleague.

Lila tried another search for "F. Knox" in Texas, since that was the address on the note, and found only one – the Frances Knox who co-authored the research paper. F. Knox, it turned out, was a woman who'd retired but still conducted experiments and crop productivity measurements for colleges and private companies. She lived in Fabens, Texas. Blackstone's note only listed Knox's Post Office box, so Lila found and wrote her physical address on a scrap of paper by the computer.

She'd found one piece of the puzzle.

Certainly, Frances Knox would have spoken with Blackstone about these seeds. She may have the whole story, the reason he'd been so excited about his project.

"Any luck?" Harry leaned over to see the computer screen.

"So far, so good. I found Frances Knox in Fabens, and she's a colleague of Dr. Blackstone."

"So, a person, then? Not a place?"

"Right."

"That's great! A person, we can ask, we can talk to about this."

"I'll see what else I can find out about the note."

"I'll leave you alone." Harry wandered back among the stacks.

She searched for the initials "PVRI" and found Prunus virginiana, the North American chokecherry, and read a short article about the plant. A wild bush or small tree found throughout the United States, it was especially common throughout the Rocky Mountain region. It produced dark purple berries that could be cooked and eaten, first used by Native Americans to make a syrup or gravy to add nutrition and flavor to dried meats. The seeds were mildly poisonous, so they were removed during cooking; unless you wanted another chokecherry plant, most people discarded them. The contents in the baggie from Blackstone matched the description of chokecherry berries with seeds in the middle. The leaves, as well, appeared to be Prunus virginiana.

What was so special about a bunch of chokecherry seeds?

CHAPTER 16

Lila rose from her chair and stretched. She could use a break from the computer screen. She hesitated, then put her phone away and lifted her pack onto her shoulder, reluctant to leave it even for a moment.

Corkboard panels stretched across the ceiling, a dusty shade of white. Signs hung from the metal framework, announcing "New Mysteries" and "Adventures." Below those, several shelves had been spaced in the open area of the building in front of the circulation desk. She wandered through the stacks, glancing at the books on display: Cave Diver, The Wreck, Steel Wind, The Measure of Ella. On another top shelf: Get Idiota, Warship Poseidon, The Internship, and books by Dirk Cussler and Wilbur Smith. On the self-help display, The Creative Heroine's Path. She'd love to lose herself in a good book, but she and Harry and Keaton were nearly done in Effington. She had a little more research to do on the computer and then maybe they could find a thrift store and then return to the highway.

She walked to the front windows, high and tinted against the afternoon sun. Beyond, she could see Keaton's blue Chevy, its chrome highlights and unique shape distinguishing it from all the other vehicles parked in the lot.

Two men began circling the antique, examining its lines, peering inside the driver's window. The car certainly did attract attention.

Then one of the men tried the door, yanking the silver handle again and again, frustration in his movements.

What?

The other man tried the doors on the other side, all of them locked. He leaned into the rear side window, cupping his hands against the glare.

These guys weren't just admiring the old car, they were trying to get inside it.

She glanced around her, searching for Harry or Keaton. A mother and her little girl moved to the main desk; books clasped to their chests like precious gifts. An elderly man sat at a table across from the computers, reading intently. Rows of shelves stood to her left, Dewey decimal numbers and topical labels pasted onto each. She strode to the first stack and began a search, moving past the rows, glancing down each one as she went. Keaton stood at the back of one set of shelves, book in hand.

She shuffled toward him. "Someone's trying to get into your car."

"What?" His hands jerked at the sound of her voice.

"Two men are trying to get into your car."

He slid the book back onto the shelf and moved past her. "Find Harry, will you?"

"Sure." She continued to the end of the row and saw Harry two stacks away.

"Harry, we need to go! Two men are trying to break into the car!"

His mouth opened, then his lips clamped tight and he swept past her in a moment. She turned and followed him toward the front desk and the big windows beyond.

Keaton stood behind a stack of new books, watching the parking lot. Lila bumped into Harry when he suddenly halted behind Keaton.

The men had left the car and were walking toward the main entrance. One was middle-aged and lean with unkempt, mousey hair and eyes spread too wide above his nose. The other had biceps the size of Lila's thighs; a weightlifter with short hair and black pupils that searched the ground like a bull on the hunt for a matador. Had the men who had killed Blackstone found them? But how could they do that?

"Time to scoot out the side," Harry touched Keaton's elbow and motioned with his chin. "Time to go."

Keaton seemed to debate the issue, but only for a moment. He nodded and looked at Lila. They moved quickly to the stacks again, Harry leading them down one row and then another and they reached a metal door with a bar across its back; "Exit" marked above the handle.

"Shit." Harry pointed to the sign below the exit marker.

"We'll set off an alarm," Keaton said.

"Should we go through it anyway?" Lila asked. The thought of being trapped released a flame of panic across her chest, heat rising to her cheeks.

CHAPTER 17

Harry peered down the nearest row of books, searching for the men.

"What do they want?" Lila asked. "Have they been following us?"

"I don't understand this." Keaton shook his head. "But," he pointed at the door, "maybe the alarm will bring the police and we can sort it."

"Wait!" Harry waived his arm. "Those guys have moved away from the front desk…"

"What?" Lila followed his gaze.

"We can go right past them, through the front door."

Her knees turned to mush.

Harry placed his hand on Keaton's shoulder. "You go first and get the car ready…"

They peered from behind the bookshelves, watching patrons meander through the display of books in the lobby. The two men had moved out of sight.

"Wait a bit, then follow me." Keaton walked stiffly into the open space, keeping his face turned toward the large windows.

Lila held her breath as Keaton strode past the circulation desk and reached the outer doors. Harry gave her a gentle nudge. She settled her daypack firmly on her shoulders and put one foot in front of the other, shuffling across the worn carpet toward the first display of books. She stopped behind the shelves and glanced around.

A mother and daughter were getting ready to leave the desk, arms filled with checked-out books. A teenage boy moved furtively from display to display, glancing at the books. She stared at the front doorway, a distance that seemed unnoticeably short when they'd arrived and now appeared impossibly far away. Lila hurried stiffly past the next display station, now about a third of the way across the large lobby.

"Oh!" She nearly collided with the teenage boy, who'd come quickly around the shelves. Instead of expressing some surprise or apology, he glared at her and spun around, heading in the opposite direction.

She stepped away from the shelves and began to cross the lobby in the open, toward the doors, when the mother and daughter team cut in front of her, forcing her to slow.

The weightlifter walked from behind a row of shelves to her left and looked directly at her, dark eyes tightened with recognition. He must have seen her in the

Chevy with Harry and Keaton. She'd become the matador, but without a spear or a cape.

She was still out in the open, behind the slow-moving mother who was headed out of the building and now directly in Lila's path.

"Come on, sweetheart." The mother turned to wait for her little girl, who struggled with her armload of books.

The man began several long strides in Lila's direction.

She spun and hurried back to the nearest display, searching for Harry. Where the hell was he?

The man angled his route to follow her.

She hurried past another display and down the first row of books, running as she entered the narrow passage. A wall of novels stood sentry at the end of the stacks, the random shades and sharpened angles of a hand-made quilt. She quickly reached the wall, her shoulder shoving into the bound volumes, redirecting her down another passage. Rows of shelves stood like columns along her right side and she sprinted past them, not daring to glance behind until she reached a blank, beige wall at the end of the stacks.

The weightlifter was nowhere in sight.

To her right, another tight pathway led through a canyon of plastic-covered spines with labels, numerals, and decimal points. She slowed herself with conscious effort, counting her inhales and exhales – in, two, three –

out, two, three.

A tall man in a black baseball cap stood where the pathway ended, running his fingers up and down the books, searching for something specific. She pretended to peruse the volumes in front of her, a customer grazing on the options. The man walked to another row and out of sight. An open staircase rose to her left and she took it on instinct, hoping to lose herself in the building.

No one else was on the stairs so she took the steps two at a time. Once past the doorway on the second level, she stopped to slow her racing heart.

Had Keaton reached the Chevy? Was he outside at this very moment with Harry, waiting for her?

Was there a second set of stairs somewhere? Or had she just fled into a room without another exit, a trap of her own making?

She hurried past the shelves to the far wall, searching for another way back to the main floor.

CHAPTER 18

Panels of glass lined the far wall and Lila moved quickly toward them. Framed in aluminum, they reminded her of schoolhouse windows, tall on the tops, with rectangular panes along the bottoms that opened outward. Florescent lights buzzed overhead like grasshoppers in a distant summer field. The path along the wall led to more rows of bookshelves and to another corner of the room, but she saw no exits other than the staircase she'd used to reach this floor.

Should she hurry back down to the main level and find an exit there?

The sound of boots climbing stairs reached her ears.

She waited there in the corner, her breath shallow, listening intently. Someone shuffled across the carpet toward the back wall, diagonally from where she stood. Then, all became quiet.

She peeked over the uneven tops of books along

the nearest shelf, seeing only one row of shelves beyond. She put one foot in front of the other, slipping carefully down the path toward the stairs, peering along a collection of American novels as she went.

Thump.

Then a man's frustrated whisper: "Damn it."

He was coming toward her, midway along the stacks, blocking the staircase.

An electrical current sizzled in some primitive part of her mind, an involuntary response to whoever stood around the corner. She spun back down the row, falling into flight as she abandoned all hope of concealment. Her palms smacked hard against the cinder block wall as she turned to her left, toward the tall windows, watching each row of books as she sped past it, seeing a blur of a man in the next stack over, cutting the distance between them.

She stopped in a corner opposite the one she'd just left, heart thumping, lungs heaving for air. The path to her left would take her straight back to the stairs and she could get there, but only if the man kept moving toward her along a different set of stacks. If he came far enough down the row he was in, she might get past him by going down another row.

She put her hands on the windowsill and tried to slow her breathing. The man must have stopped mid-stack. Or was he at the edge, ready to leap forward?

The sound of a footstep reached her ears.

The weightlifter had turned around. He was moving back toward the stairs, where he could block her escape. If he came to the end of the stacks that were straight ahead of her and turned the corner, he'd see her. He'd be only fifty feet away. If that happened, she could run down the next row, but he could run back to the stairs, blocking her again. And so, it would be an ongoing stalemate by each of them.

Maybe someone else would arrive, a legitimate patron, and she could call to them for help. But maybe the man would be faster than her, breaking the standoff.

Another shuffle against the carpet.

She glanced at the window and moved her hands to the lever that would open the lower pane. She pushed down slowly, scraping the handle against the frame until it slipped past, breaking the seal, opening the window just a crack.

She watched the end of the row, waiting, waiting for the man to leap forward and sprint toward her. The silence of the library pressed against her ears like quilting cotton.

She moved her hands slowly, pushing the window outward, gauging the length and width of the opening.

A hulk of a shadow appeared at the end of the row, not moving, not running, not reaching toward her, just standing there, observing, estimating, planning. He leaned into the light.

A smile rose on his lips.

She dropped her daypack to her feet but held it

tight with her left hand and rolled out of the open window, forcing herself through the aluminum frame.

The man began to run toward her, gaining speed as he came.

She wiggled against the frame, sliding into it, extending her legs outward and below her and she lowered quickly through until her belt snagged on something hard and it stopped her cold.

The man was nearly upon her.

She pulled her pack through the opening and tossed it behind her, down to the ground, and put both hands on the outer sill, lifting, wiggling, lifting higher and a meaty hand reached for her hair as her belt finally popped free. Her arms straightened, jarring against the concrete wall, legs kicking the air, fingertips holding her in place. As the man reached for her wrists, she let go and dropped backward into the bushes below the window frame. Branches stabbed into her shoulders, spinning her away from the building and she fell to her knees.

She heard the man's body scraping against the window frame as he grunted with effort.

He was trying to follow her.

CHAPTER 19

Lila scrambled to her feet, slinging the pack over her shoulders. She turned and looked up. The man's torso was horizontal as he struggled to squeeze through the window.

She stepped across a sidewalk and down the curb, watching her pursuer. A blur of color flashed into her periphery, and she turned to find the blue Chevy right next to her, Harry opening the door, waving her over, and she leapt inside.

Harry reached behind her and slammed the door as Keaton gassed the old engine forward and across the back lot behind the building. She slid her pack onto the floor, the three of them now side by side in the front bench seat. She reached for Harry and hugged him tight.

"You're OK." Harry patted her on the back.

She released a dry sob and squeezed his bony shoulders.

"We lost you in there," Keaton said, turning the wheel hand over hand, taking them onto the street.

She sat straight, wiped her nose, and took a shaky breath.

"Keaton picked me up," Harry said, "but we didn't see you, so we circled the building."

"Just get us the hell away from here."

Tires squeaked and momentum pressed her against the passenger door as Keaton pulled them onto a two-lane highway heading west. They were several miles south of I-70, travelling a path that was parallel to the interstate. Harry looked behind them, prompting Lila and Keaton to do the same.

No one seemed to be following them.

"What the hell?" Keaton said.

"Find us a spot to pull over, when you can," Harry replied. "I need to get something from the trunk."

Keaton looked at his friend, brow raised.

"I'll explain when we stop."

Lila clasped her hands together, one finger wrapped around the top of her daypack. "Also, I have to pee," she said meekly, eyes on the road ahead.

They drove on for another twenty minutes, still no one behind them, when a feed store with two fuel pumps appeared on an upcoming street corner. An unoccupied sheriff's truck sat by one of the gas pumps. "Canine Division" was stenciled across the pickup, but there were no dogs there. Keaton pulled in across from the truck. Lila scooted out, still grasping her pack, and found a restroom inside the store.

When she returned, Keaton had moved the car to the side of the building near two cottonwood trees. He leaned against the driver's side door, hands in his jean pockets. But for the white hair, he looked like a kid out for a cruise or a drive-in movie. Harry was rummaging in the trunk, elbows pumping, grunting something she could not quite hear.

"Let's go over there." Keaton nodded toward the trees at the edge of a barrow ditch.

They passed Harry, who said, "Be there in a minute."

Keaton walked ahead.

Lila turned to watch Harry, stepping backward as she went. He glanced around, holding something in his hands, and walked toward the empty sheriff's truck. He kept his eyes on the store inside the gas station, where the driver should be, and moved quickly to the pump next to the truck.

She slowed her steps and kept watching.

Harry dropped something into the back of the pickup, just inside the rear gate, then walked away with a practiced, casual stride. As he approached her, a man in a tan uniform left the store, fiddling with something he must have purchased. Harry continued to shuffle toward her. The deputy hopped into his truck and pulled away from the station, turning south at the intersection.

"He gone?" Harry whispered.

"Yeah, but..."

"Whew," he wiped his forehead with a touch of excess drama.

"What?"

"I'll explain," he motioned toward Keaton, who'd found a place to sit on the grass by the trees.

She turned and followed Harry and they sat in a circle, facing each other.

"First, how are you holding up?" Harry asked her. Fresh, gray whiskers had begun to carpet his cheeks and chin, making his face rougher, older. He pulled the band on his ponytail, tightening long, white hair against his skull.

"Well..." she began.

"Helluva thing," Keaton's declaration washed over them. "I mean, who the hell? And why are they after you?" He looked at Lila.

Harry cleared his throat, preparing himself. "I don't think they were after Lila, and that's good news."

Keaton's dark eyes narrowed. "What's going on here? What aren't you telling us, Harry?"

"Well, it's a bit of a story," Harry glanced at Keaton, then turned toward Lila. "You see, I know those two hoods. They work for Johnny McCarthy."

"Shit," Keaton said.

"Who's that?" she asked.

"Johnny's a hoodlum of the worst variety. We grew

up with him," Keaton pointed to himself and Harry, "went to high school with him. Hangs with a drug dealer who did two stints in Michigan City."

Lila squinted; her question implicit.

"It's the state prison. Famous for holding John Dillinger in the 30s," Keaton said. "So why are two of Johnny's goons after us? It's not for the old Chevy…"

"No," Harry looked to the grass at his feet. "I got in some trouble, Keaton, and Johnny bailed me out…"

"I don't like the sound of this," Keaton leaned forward, his features hard.

"Well, I didn't like the sound of it, either, but I owe Johnny some money and a favor and, well, I really didn't want to tell you this, 'cause I know how you are about it…"

"Drugs!" Keaton rose quickly to his feet, fists clenched. "You're in some kind of drug deal, aren't you, Harry?"

CHAPTER 20

"Wait, Keaton," Lila looked up at him, a plea in her eyes. "Let's hear him out…"

Keaton crossed his arms and waited.

"OK, here it is. You remember that medical marijuana shop in Ohio I was supplying for a while? Well, the shop went under, and the pot disappeared – somebody stole it – and I still owed Johnny for half of it…"

"…how much?" Keaton asked.

"…six grand…"

Keaton huffed.

"…and Johnny agreed I could work it off, pay him back in full with a delivery – just one delivery – to a contact near El Paso."

"So just where is this pot?"

"The two green dry bags in the trunk."

"Shit."

"When you decided to go to El Paso to sell your

Chevy, that was perfect, so…"

"And you decided not to tell me." Keaton forced his words through tightened lips, each syllable on a leash.

"To protect you, Keaton. You don't know about it, so if something goes wrong, it's all on me. That's why I didn't want you to know."

"And because I'd have said no way in hell."

"This really helps me out of a jam with Johnny and hey, Keaton, it's only pot. It's going legal soon, completely legal, and the market for us independents is going to dry up in the next couple of years. It's a low-risk deal that will get me even with Johnny once and for all."

"Wait. What does that have to do with those men chasing me?" Lila interrupted, her question aimed at Harry.

"They work for Johnny."

"Were they the ones chasing us in that brown car a while back? On the country roads?" she asked.

"Don't know. I couldn't see who was in that car," Harry said.

"But…why would they be after us? I mean, what do they want?" she turned her palms upward as if waiting to catch the answer.

"Right," Harry leaned toward her. "Good question. Did Johnny decide he couldn't trust me? Are they making sure I complete the delivery? But that makes no sense. I mean, it would cost Johnny money to have them following us."

"And they were doing more than following." She looked at each of them.

"Yeah," Keaton lowered his arms.

"If Johnny had wanted his goons to deliver the pot, he could have just given it to them." Harry folded his fingers together.

"They're trying to steal the pot from Johnny," Keaton's eyes widened.

"Bingo. That's what I think, too," Harry said.

"Great, Harry, that's just super – now we have two thieves on our tails, and we don't know what they'll try next." His sentence was an equal mix of sarcasm and disdain.

Harry drove a puff of air from his lungs, a defensive response.

Lila looked from one man to the other. "This has nothing to do with Dr. Blackstone's murder?"

"Probably not." Harry shook his head.

"So, you've put all of us in danger, Harry…"

"No, but here's the thing. How do you think they found us? We're in a small-town library at supper time and they just happen to pull into the parking lot and see the car?"

Keaton and Lila looked at each other.

"Johnny had GPS beacons in each of the bags, so he could track our progress across the country. His gorillas knew that. All they had to do was look us up and be there whenever we stopped." Harry brushed a hair behind his ear. "That's why I got rid of them."

"What?"

"I dropped the beacons in the back of that sheriff's truck. They'll be following the canine unit for a while and when they finally catch up to him, when they realize it, it will be too late. We're already long gone and away from them."

"You think that fixes this?" Keaton asked.

"Well..."

"You lied to me," Keaton pointed at Harry.

"No, never."

"You kept it hidden from me."

"To keep you safe, to keep you out of it."

"You knew I'd say no, and you did it anyway."

"No..."

"This is the real reason you didn't want Lila to call the police, isn't it?" he jabbed a finger toward Harry.

"No." He twisted another blade of grass.

"You know, your brother would never have done something like this."

Harry turned aside, a grimace on his lips, and for four dense seconds his eyes glistened with moisture, the blood drained from his cheeks.

Keaton stared into the evening sky, eyes darkened by storm.

A heavy silence drained the oxygen from the air.

Keaton turned with a slow, measured resolve and walked away.

CHAPTER 21

Wormwood hung up the desk phone and drew a deep breath. He'd bargained hard on the call and reached a deal with his inside source: eight percent of the revenue for the first four years, minus direct expenses. Hell, he'd have gone to fifteen percent for five years. He'd already taken the critical first steps toward getting Dr. Blackstone's seeds and now he'd nailed down a key part of the rest of it. He'd call the patent attorneys in the morning and get them started on the process, prime them for success. His lips climbed into a smile then dropped again.

He still had to get the seeds.

And how far could he really trust his source? They'd betrayed Blackstone, after all.

"Mr. Wormwood," his secretary's voice blared from the intercom. "Your wife is on line two."

He took a moment then tucked the receiver between his shoulder and chin. "Hey, baby, how's your day going?"

"Good, hon. I know you're busy at work, but I just had lunch with Gloria and Stephan…" she said, her voice full of optimism.

"Yes?"

"Well, I know we've had to tighten our belts lately, but they've invited us on a wonderful trip to Hawaii…"

He released a stream of air.

"No, listen for a moment. In eight weeks, they're flying to Waikiki and have two rooms reserved at a beautiful hotel right on the beach. We'd stay there three days, swim in the ocean, check out the shops, relax. Maybe take a sailboat ride, a sunset tour. Then, this is the big news, they have these friends with a condo on Maui and we can stay with them – for free! We'd take a helicopter ride to the big island and have five full days there! Island tours, horseback riding…"

"…you know I'm allergic…"

"Or you could go parasailing…"

"…you see me parasailing?"

"Or whatever, but we can rest and swim and drink mai tais on the beach!"

The phone slipped from under his chin, and he raised his shoulder to keep it in place.

"Alice…"

"Keith…" He heard the small plea in her voice.

"Baby, we're right in the middle of something really big right now."

"You'll be done with it in a few weeks, won't you? You'll really need a vacation then." Her voice hardened. "And I need a vacation, hon. I mean, we haven't had a big trip for three years."

"We went to Lake Michigan last year, that cabin on the lake…"

He felt the silence on the other end of the line.

They'd had this conversation off and on for nearly two years, since Dragontree's income dipped, since they'd had to sell the townhouse in Belize. He knew that Alice had hoped for more from him and instead of gaining ground, they'd been losing it.

She needed a vacation and he had to admit, she was right. He needed one, too. And Hawaii had always been high on her list.

He slid the phone into his hand, squeezing it tight. "Hon…"

He heard a quick sniffle on the other end of the line.

Alice had been raised in mid-level luxury, her father a hedge fund manager with two homes, a ninety-five-foot yacht, a new Mercedes every other year. She'd earned a degree in journalism, but even in college, her father paid for tuition and an upscale apartment. She hadn't had to work weekends or between classes and she'd taken two whole semesters on European cruise liners – travel was in her blood. Alice was just not built for middle income, let alone poverty.

"I've got a budget worked out for the trip…" Her

voice trailed into silence.

Damn it. He leaned back, nose high, breath deep, as if he were smelling the air.

"Listen, baby, I've got a great project going now that could put us back on top. Let's be optimistic. Let's plan for the trip and unless the bottom falls out, we'll go."

"For sure, this time?"

"For sure this time." He squeezed the phone until his knuckles turned white and he knew he'd just committed, regardless of the success of his bid for the missing seeds.

He heard a short squeal on the line. "I've got to tell Gloria and Stephan, right away, hon."

"I've gotta run, so I'll see you tonight."

"I love you."

"You too." He placed the phone back in its cradle and stared at the bookcase against the wall.

He had the investigative team on the job, scanning their contacts in the business, scouring the country. But this was not something he could do remotely anymore. A corkscrew smile rose on his lips.

Wormwood moved to the safe he kept behind his desk, a two-foot by two-foot chunk of metal he rarely used. His knees crackled when he bent to the floor. He spun the dial until the latch broke free, then reached inside, pulled a snub-nosed .38 from the shelf and pocketed a box of ammunition.

He was joining the search for those goddammed seeds himself.

CHAPTER 22

"He should never have brought up my brother like that…" Harry watched his friend walk away.

"You guys…it seems like you've been pals forever." Lila leaned toward him. "Have you?"

"Yeah." Harry took a breath. "Since high school, like me and Johnny. Well, not exactly like that…"

She tilted her head, seeking an explanation.

"Keaton is about two years older than me. He and my brother Leo were in Afghanistan together. Infantry. They were brothers-in-arms. Leo was killed by an IED on a trail they were on near Nangalam, Northeast of Kabul."

"I'm so sorry…"

"Yeah, twenty-two years ago still feels like twenty-two hours. Anyway," he shook his head, pushing the memory aside, "when Keaton came home, we sort of adopted each other, you know? We have a brother in common, Keaton and me."

She put her hand on his arm.

"I'm protecting Keaton from my deal with Johnny. I will always protect him. I'll swear he never knew anything about it. He's home-run safe. I don't see why he's so pissed. And it's not that much farther to get to El Paso, where I can get rid of the pot forever."

Harry worked his jaw in a circle, lips clamped like he had captured a batch of bees inside. She watched him patiently, inviting him to say what else might be on his mind.

He glanced at the ground.

"It has to be truly frustrating," she said.

"Well, it is. And Lila," he looked at her closely, "I need to get out from under the debt with Johnny, but there's something else, too. I also need the money..."

She waited.

His face slowly relaxed, a pair of parentheses bordering a nascent smile. "Don't laugh, but I plan to open my own bookshop. It's seed money to get me started. Keaton doesn't consider how important this is to me."

"That's wonderful!" she beamed, then let her expression drop. "Does Keaton know about the bookstore?"

Harry's eyes focused on the blue horizon. "Well... now that you say that..."

She let Harry settle into his thoughts.

Right from the start, these old friends had saved her, and they'd been generous and supportive well beyond what they'd had to do. And they were more than just friends. She hated seeing them at odds with each other.

"Is there some way to resolve this problem between you and Keaton?"

"No. He's stubborn as a mule and half as smart. He thinks 'smoking weed is the devil's deed,' so the saying goes. When he gets in this mood, there's not much anyone can do."

"Oh."

"Listen," Harry motioned toward her with his chin. "Maybe we can drop you somewhere safe, where you can get a bus or something…"

"No, please, that's not what I want. I really need your help – from both of you guys."

"I'm not sure how much longer I'll be of any help to either of you. I don't have a car, so I can't take you to El Paso. And I need to avoid the police for a few more days and deliver the pot like I promised."

"Right now, I'm not sure I want to deal with police, either," she said.

Harry raised his brow.

"I didn't tell you this before, but I'm a Canadian citizen, here on a student visa…"

"I thought I detected a slight accent."

"I grew up in Michigan almost as much as in Toronto. Anyway, the problem is, my visa requires me to only work on-campus. When Dr. Blackstone advertised for summer help, I jumped at it. It was a great opportunity. I hadn't thought about the off-campus rule until a friend of mine nearly got deported for the same thing."

"That's crazy."

"I guess they don't want us 'aliens' taking jobs from U.S. citizens." Her lips tightened into an ironic smile. She shrugged a sad resignation, like she'd just been banned from her best friends' club on a technicality.

"But you're a student here." Harry's back straightened. "How do they expect you to survive without a job?"

"You can ask for a variance – an exception to the rule – but you have to ask in advance. Now I'll have to ask after the fact and the one man I thought could smooth it over for me, well…he's been murdered."

"We've gotta find a way to help you," Harry insisted.

"You've got a problem of your own." She motioned toward Keaton.

Harry grumbled deep in his throat.

CHAPTER 23

Lila wondered if getting these guys to focus on Dr. Black-stone's murder and the chokecherry seeds could help get them back on track.

"Let me talk to him…" She stood and walked to Keaton, who was pacing behind one of the cottonwoods. As she approached, he stopped and waited.

"I'm sorry you got mixed up in this." He leaned against the tree.

"It's all right."

"No, Harry's been connected with Johnny since high school, and that guy is all trouble." He shook his head. "Johnny's a big pot farmer – always has been. Distributer, too. Guys he runs with sell harder stuff, too, sometimes. Even meth."

She shook her head.

"That shit comes straight from hell."

"I know."

"Harry knows better than to borrow from that thug. He knows better." Keaton pushed his toe into the dirt.

"Yeah, I can see that. But once he did, Johnny had his hooks into him."

"That's exactly what I mean."

"So his mistake was borrowing money from the guy. Trusting him a little bit. Now he has to deliver that pot, or he'll be in worse trouble. But once he does, he's out of debt, free and clear."

"Free to do this all over again."

She touched his hand.

"And now it's your problem, too," he said.

"No, I've got my own, even if you don't count Dr. Blackstone's murder." She explained her student visa issue to Keaton, who clicked his tongue at the off-campus rule. "But listen, I hate to see anything get between you guys. He really messed up, but his heart's in the right place, as my grandma used to say."

"Don't know about that." His eyelids narrowed.

"Well, I'm still in deep shit and none of it is Harry's fault or yours. I've no right to ask this, after all you guys have done for me already, but…"

He straightened.

"I still really need your help. Whoever murdered Dr. Blackstone might be after me now, if they can find me. I still need to figure out why. I've got a god-forsaken bag of chokecherry seeds. I still don't know why Blackstone wanted them sent to Frances Knox, whoever she really is. And I've still got to get to El Paso, or south of there, and do it quickly because if the government finds out I've been violating the rules and I'm connected to a murder, they'll deport me in a flash. So, I have a question."

"Yes?"

"It's a selfish one and I have no right to ask."

He nodded, a gesture that she should proceed.

"Just for now, can we get in your trusty Bel Air and find a restaurant somewhere along the highway and have a solid meal? The sun is setting, I'm exhausted and starving, and I need you guys to help me figure out what to do." She lowered her voice. "And if you need to leave me, please leave me somewhere where I can catch a bus."

Keaton stared into the cottonwood overhead, its leaves shaking on gangly stems. He held his fingers to the bridge of his nose and pinched, and shook his head, then looked at her. "You're right about one thing. The marijuana isn't your problem."

"You guys have been so nice to me, so sweet. But if I can just get to a bigger city, somewhere I can catch another ride to El Paso..."

"He's put me in a terrible spot, you know. But no matter what he's done…I don't want to just leave him in the middle of nowhere. He'll get busted for sure." He rubbed his forehead. "Can you imagine Harry living in prison?"

"I don't want to."

"Let's go talk with him."

They moved back to where Harry was sitting. He'd plucked blades of grass from the ground and was mangling them in his fingers.

Keaton sighed. "Here's the deal. It's late and we're hungry. I can drop you at a bus station tomorrow, but in the meantime, we need to keep moving."

Oh, dear. She looked at her feet, lips clamped with regret. They're going to separate…and the idea of leaving her at a bus station just got transformed into leaving Harry at one, instead.

"All right, Keaton, but how about this." Harry dropped the blades of grass. "Let's take the back roads to St. Louis and Interstate 44 and drive through the night to Oklahoma City. You can leave me there."

Keaton shook his head. "Let's go north to I-70 instead."

Were these two going to disagree out of spite?

Harry's eyes narrowed. "That's not the direct route to El Paso. If we take Interstate 44, cut southwest from Missouri, down through Oklahoma, it'll shorten the drive."

"Harry," Keaton looked from under his brow, "that's why I-70 is a good idea. If Johnny's guys try to get ahead of us, and they will, they'll do it on route 44. So, I take it straight west to Colorado instead, then go south. It's a little longer, but I also know a guy near Chugaro, in the southern corner of the state. It would be safer…" He glanced at Lila, a silent message to Harry that the two of them should focus on what was best for her.

"Oh, yeah…of course." He stood and brushed the dust from his pants. "North to I-70 it is."

Would Harry be taking a bus in the morning? If so, how was he going to keep all that pot from being discovered?

"And for Lila's sake," Keaton said, "let's get some food in our bellies."

CHAPTER 24

They travelled northwest to Vandalia, almost four hours of driving, and stopped for a restroom break and food at an Arby's at nearly seven o'clock in the evening. Harry and Keaton had reached some sort of uncomfortable détente, speaking to each other politely but only as necessary. When Harry was in the men's room, Keaton told Lila he thought there might not be a regular bus depot in Vandalia and probably no bus to catch at that hour, anyway. She didn't volunteer to check the internet for information that might contradict his assumption.

He seemed resigned to taking Harry at least a little farther, maybe as a compromise between the position each of them had taken back where Harry had dropped the GPS devices in the sheriff's canine unit truck.

Harry bought two coffees and drove into the night, through St. Louis and into Missouri. They stopped for gas and Lila wandered the convenience store isles, stopping to stare at a pair of chocolate cupcakes wrapped in cellophane. No, she thought, then picked them up, squeezing an imprint of her thumb into the icing. Her mind felt like it was going backwards, fatigue warping her sense of direction. She took a step toward the counter to pay when a man moved in front of her, his bulk vaguely familiar.

The man who'd chased her in the library? How could that be?

She stepped back quickly.

But then he glanced at her and smiled, his face clean and friendly.

Just another traveler. He paid for tea and a pack of peanuts and left.

She'd squeezed one of the cakes nearly in half.

They stopped two more times through the night for gas and restrooms. Keaton offered to drive but Harry bought two more coffees near Independence and stayed with it, skirting around Kansas City and far across the state to a little spot called Ogallah, nearly nine more hours of driving time. Lila lay restlessly in the back seat, rocking on the old shocks, highway lights flashing like meteors across her vision until sleep finally pulled her into its slippery grip.

She woke when the Chevy had slowed, taking turns that tugged her one way, then another. Gravel fired like popcorn under the tires until they lurched to a full stop, her bones still vibrating with the road. The front doors opened, turning on the cabin light above, an annoying reminder that, apparently, she needed to get up.

"What time is it?" She sat upright, combing her hair with her fingers.

"Almost two in the morning," Keaton kept his voice just above a whisper. "We found a little park so we're going to sack out."

She put her feet on the floor and reached for a bottle of water. The trunk opened wide, the men pulling things out, rocking the car.

"Here," Harry said, handing blankets to her across the front seat.

"Give her a sleeping bag, Harry," Keaton scolded.

"What?" Harry stopped.

Lila took the blankets from him. "These will do just fine."

"See?" Harry said to Keaton.

She spoke through tightened lips. "What are we going to do, guys, bicker all night?"

"You stay where you are. We'll sleep in our sleeping bags next to the car, on the grass," Harry said.

"Public restroom over there." Keaton pointed behind him.

She tumbled from the car, used the lady's room, then crawled back inside. The air was cold, and she quickly gathered under the blankets and lay back. Within moments, a network of English ivy, Hedera helix, had spread across her dreams.

****

Male voices tugged her into the waking world, the sound of one of them in particular. His words were clipped and to the point. Professional.

She sat up but kept the blanket over her chest.

"I didn't see a sign," Harry said.

A county sheriff, uniform tight across his shoulders, pointed to a sign about twenty feet away.

"Oh."

"No overnight camping," the deputy said.

"Sorry, officer, I didn't see it. We came in about two this morning, and I just didn't see it," Harry shrugged.

The deputy's hair was cut close, his limbs long and lanky. He turned at the waist, hands on a belt loaded with gear, full of Batman-style gadgets, she supposed. He looked through the window, brown eyes staring straight into hers.

Lila smiled at the man, pushing the surprise from her face. She combed her fingers through her hair, working to get fully awake.

"Who else is with you, sir?" the deputy asked.

"My friend, Keaton."

"And where is he?" The deputy shifted away from Harry, looking around the picnic grounds.

Harry widened his eyes at Lila, a message that panic hid beneath a thin veneer.

Keaton walked toward the Chevy from the restrooms, towel across his shoulder, ready for the day. Harry and the deputy turned to watch him.

Lila pulled her toothbrush and comb from her pack and slid out of the car. Keaton nodded a quick greeting to the officer. Lila said "good morning" to the three men, her voice a touch less assured than she'd intended.

The deputy looked at her. "Are you all right, ma'am?"

"A little sleepy." Lila shifted her feet.

"No, I mean, are you all right?" His voice dropped an octave and he lowered his brow. "Is everything here all right with you?"

"Oh," she straightened her back. "Of course, sheriff." She squeezed her grip on the toothbrush.

"You're the driver?" He turned back to Harry, who seemed to be controlling his breath in smooth, even draws.

"Last night I was driving, but we've been taking turns. Keaton owns the car."

Keaton's pupils seemed blackened with concern, a detail she hoped the officer would not notice. He stepped closer and offered his hand to the deputy, who gave it a quick shake.

"We're driving cross country to deliver this," he pointed to the Chevy, "to a shop that restores antique cars."

The deputy looked at each of them, questions unasked. "I need your license, registration, and proof of insurance."

"Of course." Keaton opened the passenger door

and rooted through the glove box as he spoke. "She needs new shocks, a little rust work…" he handed papers to the deputy, "…but she runs well, and I'd like to see her restored, you know, staying on the roads."

The deputy examined the documents. Harry handed him his driver's license. Lila went back to her pack and pulled out her wallet.

When the officer had seen all of their licenses, he returned them and began moving around the car, looking inside. "You're a vet?" he asked Keaton. "It's on your driver's license…"

"Infantry, Afghanistan," Keaton said. "Honorable discharge."

The deputy nodded, continuing his examination as he walked toward the rear bumper. "Please open the trunk, sir."

CHAPTER 25

Lila's stomach seemed to drop to her feet.

Harry plastered a grin on his lips that twisted to a minor grimace, a sign of the exertion needed to swallow his protest.

The officer rested one hand on his belt, the other against his shoulder, fingers slightly cupped as if holding an imaginary nightstick or a rifle.

Keaton's muscles tensed for a split second, his brown eyes flashing a sideways glance at Lila, then Harry. He took a breath, then opened like a flowering plant in time-lapse photography, his shoulders relaxing, a deep smile blooming on his face.

"Sure thing, officer." Keaton walked to the trunk. "Where did you serve?"

The deputy looked at him. "How did you know?"

"Just something we soldiers notice." Keaton pulled the key from his pocket. "Army?"

"Reserve."

They exchanged a quick nod.

"Just have to give this latch a little jiggle." Keaton twisted then popped open the trunk and stepped back.

The deputy leaned in, glancing left and right.

"Help yourself, sir." Keaton pointed. "Clothes, tools, water jugs, tarp to cover the car when we're not driving…"

"This thing is huge." He twisted at the waist, facing Keaton.

"Yeah," Keaton chuckled. "They built 'em big back then. This is a '60 Bel Air. We rebuilt the engine 'bout three years ago." His words betrayed some pride. "Let me show you under the hood, officer. There's so much room in there, you can climb in and sit on the wheel well to check the spark plugs."

The deputy hesitated, then stepped back from the trunk.

Keaton slammed the lid shut and they walked to the front of the car.

Harry turned his back to them for a moment, thankful eyes aimed at the gods above. Lila focused on the ground and scratched her forehead, a smirk rising behind the palm of her hand.

Keaton displayed the engine compartment to the deputy, and they leaned deep inside, teenage boys wide-eyed at the notion of exploding gasoline, grown men surprised at the ingenuity of a design that worked without computer sensors or micro-chips.

"See how simple it is?" Keaton pointed at various component parts, giving the officer a brief tour.

After a few more moments, they stood clear and Keaton shoved the hood down and closed, adding his weight to secure the latch.

"Folks, I'm going to let this go with a warning." The deputy hooked his thumbs into his belt, a slight swagger of authority. "But you can't stay here tonight, so you'd best find a proper camping site from now on."

"Of course, officer." Keaton nodded.

Harry and Lila smiled their gratitude.

"You folks have a nice day," he started away then turned his head toward them. "And keep yourselves and that antique safe."

"Will do." Keaton waved, and the deputy walked to his unit and drove away.

Harry smiled like a lottery winner and patted Keaton on the back. "Very cool. I didn't know you had that in you, man." They were the first friendly words he'd said to Keaton since early the day before.

Keaton nodded, his tone flat: "Victory is often achieved by misdirection." He moved to the grassy area and began rolling up his sleeping bag.

Harry stepped toward Lila and crossed his arms. "Now he's quoting The Art of War," he mused, his voice but a whisper.

"Really?" she asked.

"That's how he frames things, but…"

She stepped closer to hear him better.

"He thinks I achieved a victory by lying to him. It tells me he's still mad as hell." Harry's eyes glazed against the morning light and his chin bobbed downward, a subtle resignation. He turned to gather his own sleeping bag, leaving Lila to wonder what might be next between these two old friends.

CHAPTER 26

Harry opened the breeze wing on his side of the car, the 60s rendition of air conditioning. They drove without conversation, travelling west to Colby, Kansas, situated along I-70.

They found a local café that advertised the world's greatest raspberry pie and pulled off the highway. They soon slowed behind a cattle drive of sorts, cows ambling down the main street, wandering left and right, dropping fresh patties onto the pavement. Cowboys kept them moving along, spurring their horses now and then, startling the calves with a shout or a rawhide slap.

"Traffic jam," Harry pointed at the reluctant bovine. "Small town style."

Keaton parked the royal blue Chevy by a row of windows and found a booth away from others. A distracted waitress in a gray uniform took their orders: two egg burritos, scrambled eggs, sausage, potatoes, coffee, one Pepsi.

"Make it a diet," Harry told the young waitress. "Balances out the taters." Her lips rose in a tired smile, and she went to fill their orders.

Lila folded her hands on the table-top, determined to start the conversation before either of them had the chance to screw it up. She had to focus – they all had to focus – on the biggest problem at hand. "Would you guys help me go over what we know so far about Dr. Blackstone's murder and those chokecherry seeds?"

"Good idea," Keaton nodded. "Start us off…"

"Right. We don't know any more about the murder itself. But at the library, we figured out what 'F. Knox' was – a person, not a place. She's a colleague of Blackstone's in a town just south of El Paso. I got that just by putting the words in the search along with the mailing address on the note from my boss."

"Didn't you find something else about a tree?"

"Yeah, the American sweetgum tree. The note says that IRGA indicates plus or minus 374,000 kilograms per year per adult plant sequestration and that that is about 984% more than what a sweetgum sequesters."

"What's IRGA, again?" Harry asked.

"IRGA is an infra-red gas analyzer. It compares the CO_2 passing into a chamber surrounding a leaf or plant and the CO_2 passing out of the chamber. It allows you to figure out the amount of CO_2 that's absorbed by the leaves of a plant."

They watched a woman herd three small children through the restaurant door, spinning, catching, redirecting them to a table at the other end of the café.

"So, is 374,000 whatever you call it a really high number? Or a really low number?" Keaton leaned forward.

"High. Really high. The note says it's 985% more than what a sweetgum tree absorbs, and the sweetgum is already one of the highest absorbers of CO_2."

Keaton rubbed the beard beneath his lip.

Harry stared at the table like it was the mirror in Alice in Wonderland.

She wondered what Dr. Blackstone would have said about all of this.

"Do you need to do more research?" Harry asked.

Keaton moved his arms off the table as the waitress arrived. The smell of grilled sausage, cheese, and eggs disrupted their discussion, their mouths soon stuffed with hot, fresh food. They ate without speaking, reveling in steaming protein, sweet ketchup, crunchy fries.

"Oh my god, I was starving," Lila said as she picked at what was left of her potatoes.

Harry and Keaton grunted in agreement.

She pulled her cell phone from her pack and turned it on. "Still charged up from when we were at the library," she said, tapping at the keys, swiping across the screen.

Keaton released a shallow belch.

"And we've got a decent signal here."

"I'm still not sure what this is really about," Harry said.

"We humans are pumping about fifty-one billion tons of greenhouse gas into the atmosphere each year," she said. "Too much of it poisons the climate."

"That much I know. We're headed to the edge of a cliff." Harry's lips hardened.

Lila scratched her temple. "I don't know if it's about that or not. Plants absorb CO_2 in varying degrees. Most scientists have concluded that growing more trees is not going to save the planet, though."

"Why not?" Keaton asked.

"Well, the amounts absorbed are way too small. For example, it would take a forest eight times the size of England to absorb all the CO_2 the country is producing. Plus, it takes years for trees to grow to maturity. Then, when they die and decay, they release that same CO_2 back into the atmosphere."

"But a tree that absorbs almost 1,000 times what the sweetgum tree absorbs?" Harry took a sip of his coffee.

"Right. I don't know. If we take the England example, a forest of chokecherries would not have to be eight times the size of the country."

Keaton's eyes rolled toward his brow as if reading something in the fold. "When you multiply something by a thousand, you move the decimal point three spaces to the right. Eight becomes 8,000. When you divide something by a thousand, you move the decimal point three spaces to the left. Eight becomes .008."

"Correct," Lila agreed. "The area would have to be .008 times the size of the country. Let's see…" she tapped into the computer on her phone, stopped, started again, and stared at the screen.

"Yeah?" Keaton asked.

"I was checking on the size of England, which is about 32 million acres. Eight times that size is 256 million acres but .008 times 32 million is only 256,000 acres. About 4 million acres of England is already forested." She squinted at the calculator function on her phone, entering numbers. "It would require only about 6.4 percent of the existing forested area to be populated with the new breed of chokecherry to counter-balance what England releases each year in CO_2."

"Shit," Harry spit a mouthful back into his mug. "Your Dr. Blackstone developed a plant that would do that?"

Her mouth hung open a moment. "The note said, 'magic beans.'"

"So, this is about climate change?" Harry asked.

Keaton straightened.

"These plants wouldn't solve the problem completely." She shook her head. "You can't just replace 6.4 percent of the trees on the planet with chokecherries. And it would take a few years to maximize the benefit."

"But those bushes grow fast. And get as big as little trees," Harry said.

"And they live a long time," she added. "They're hardy and they grow pretty much all over North America and all over the world."

"So, they'll be cheap to grow," Keaton said.

"We still have to stop using carbon-based energy, all around the world, and drop our CO_2 production dramatically."

"But a bush that can do that? Reduce the required acres of an area to .008 times that area?" Harry said.

They sat staring at their empty plates, the muffled voices and treble clangs of the busy café oddly out of place.

"It may not save the planet from the apes," Harry joked, pointing to the three of them, "but it might slow global warming long enough for us to change our ways. Long enough to do all the other things we have to do."

"So, are these bushes really worth enough money for someone to murder Dr. Blackstone to get them?" Keaton asked.

Lila spread her hands wide. "An antidote against the poison? It's gotta be worth millions."

CHAPTER 27

The waitress refilled their mugs, and they sipped their bitter drinks, distracted by Dr. Blackstone's vital discovery and what it might mean for the planet. Lila's thoughts eventually returned to the murder, and she remembered speaking with Mr. Jones.

"Hey, guys, I promised to call Wayland Jones again." She looked for his number on her phone.

"Wait." Harry reached across the table. "Do you trust him?"

"Why wouldn't I?"

"He's with the government."

"I'm not that paranoid," she said, immediately regretting her choice of words.

"I'm not paranoid," Harry said, "but just because he's with the feds doesn't mean he's trustworthy, either."

Keaton's index fingers rose like a conductor's, in control of the music. "Consider this, Lila: Dr. Blackstone didn't trust him."

"What?" She put her phone down.

"Wait, you agree with me?" Harry gawked at Keaton.

"Even a broken clock is right twice a day," he quipped.

OMG. If these two mules didn't stop nipping at each other, she was going to blow a gasket.

Keaton turned back to Lila. "Blackstone gave you those seeds to send to Knox. Whatever reasons he had, he had them. If you give them to Jones..." he shrugged. "Maybe it's not a matter of trusting Jones. It's a matter of trusting Blackstone. Maybe Knox will know exactly the right thing to do, and Jones won't know, or he won't be able to do the right thing because of his boss or some kind of federal regulations."

She slumped in her seat, deflated.

"You should do whatever you think is right," Harry said. "I gave you my two cents, but sometimes that's all it's worth."

"That goes for me, too," Keaton added. "Call him, like you promised. Tell him you're OK, but you don't have to tell him where you're going. Unless you want to."

"Why shouldn't I tell him we're going to see Knox?"

Keaton frowned. "Blackstone didn't tell Jones about Knox."

"Then I should be calling Knox, but I don't have her number. It wasn't on the internet site I saw at the library."

"You could try again - your phone's charged up now," Harry said.

Their waitress arrived and began clearing plates from the table. Keaton asked for a cup of coffee to go but Harry and Lila declined anything more from the menu. Lila watched the waitress balance plates on her forearms then load her hands with more.

"I'm going to call Jones and let him know I'm OK, but that's all." She punched his number into her phone and on the fourth ring, he answered.

"Lila?"

"I'm here. Just calling you back, like I said."

"You're OK?"

"Sure."

"Thank god."

"What's going on? Anything new?"

"The office and greenhouse are still locked down, of course. The sheriff is looking for you, for questioning. I told him I might be able to find you and talk you into coming back."

She waited a beat. "Well, I'm still travelling right now." She glanced at Harry and Keaton.

"Listen, Lila, I can use my contacts to help smooth things over for you here, but you really need to come back."

"I will, just not yet. Do they have any idea who would have shot Dr. Blackstone?" A lump formed in her throat as she said his name.

"No and we're racking our brains over it here. Was there anyone he might have angered?"

"I don't know…"

"Where are you now? When will you be back? If I can tell the sheriff that, he might get off my back and relax a bit. If you won't let me help you, the man is ready to put out a nation-wide man hunt."

"Oh, no. I didn't think… I mean…"

"That's OK, but if you don't help me with something, I can't stop the man. He's like a dog on a bone, you know?"

She looked from Keaton to Harry. "I'm heading west, to the Rocky Mountains for a bit of hiking. I may be off the radar a little while longer."

"Well…" She heard the disappointment in his voice. "That's something I can tell him, I guess. You're travelling and hiking, not running away..."

"That's right."

"Did Dr. Blackstone give you anything, by any chance?"

Her throat thickened and she held her breath a beat. "What would he give to me?"

"I don't know, I'm just asking. Police here are looking for a motive and they're pretty damn curious why you're not around."

"Listen, my ride is leaving, so I've gotta go."

"OK, but call me again and keep in touch so I can

tell the sheriff."

"Will do." She disconnected from the call, wondering whether she was doing the right thing.

CHAPTER 28

She tucked her phone into her pack, pondering her call with Jones and glanced around the café, eyes lingering on the entrance. "Hey, Keaton," Lila whispered. "Do the police use bounty hunter types to find someone they want to interview?"

"What?"

"Those guys…" she nodded toward the front door.

Two men had walked in, T-shirts tight against their muscles, one with a black leather vest, one with a faded jean jacket. One looked directly at Lila, Harry, and Keaton, pointing at them.

Their table was in a corner of the restaurant. There was nowhere they could go to avoid these men.

Two highway patrolmen walked into the café and stood behind the men who'd been watching Lila. The men glanced at the officers and stiffened, then moved quietly toward Lila's table.

Harry turned in his seat, watching them approach.

The first man had pin-prick eyes and a pinched nose twisted at the bridge like a key, half-turned. Patches with letters and designs spread across the shoulders of his coat, one with a black-on-white motorcycle, one with a military rifle, but she couldn't read what they said. He marched straight to the table and stopped.

The second man was bigger than the first, his nose a crooked piece of fruit, his lips a slash above a rugged chin.

The first man lay his palms on the table, knuckles calloused and etched with automotive grease. "You guys own that '60 Chevy out there?"

"Sure do," Keaton said.

The second man stared at Lila a bit too long, then glanced from Harry to Keaton and broke into a broad smile, cheeks rising, eyes crinkling, suddenly a friendly neighbor. "Sweet ride, my friend."

"Yeah," Harry nodded.

"That's a Bel Air, right? Not an Impala?"

"Right."

"I grew up working on one of those monsters," the first man said. "Any chance she's for sale?"

"No," Keaton shook his head. "Already sold. We're on our way to deliver it."

"Damn," the first man said, crossing his arms, shaking his head.

"Well, folks, sorry to bother you, but we just had to ask," the second man said. "You got a real beauty there."

"Thanks, guys," Keaton said.

"Safe travels," the first man waved. They turned and walked down the aisle toward the other side of the café.

"Shit," Lila heard herself say.

"Relax, would you?" Harry touched her shoulder, then quickly added, "But let's get out of this café."

They left the little restaurant, shuffling across the graveled lot to the Chevy. She didn't see the men who had approached them inside. Harry walked to the passenger side of the car, put his hands on the roof, and looked at Keaton.

"Look, I've been thinking a lot about this...disagreement." Harry motioned toward Keaton and himself. "I'm sure I can catch a bus at Colby, maybe an hour's drive from here. Hell, I probably could have found a depot back in Hays, but I appreciate you letting me get a little farther along. If you'll get me to Colby, though, I'll take my green dry bags and buy a bus ticket to Texas."

Lila felt the scrambled eggs take a tumble in her stomach.

"Works for me," Keaton said.

"Wait, you guys, hold on a second." She adjusted the strap on her daypack. "You can't really be serious?"

"I've done what I could to protect him, but he doesn't trust me anymore," Harry said to her.

"Protect me?" Keaton's voice rose. "From your own bad decisions?"

"I've got good reasons to make this run to El Paso..."

"…guys…"

"What?" They spoke over themselves, voices irate, heads turned toward her.

She felt the heat rise in her cheeks and a dizziness surge through her forehead like she'd suddenly arrived on a wind-blown mountain summit. Her hands clenched into fists, and she drew a deep breath, banishing the wooziness by sheer determination. "I thought we were a team, the three of us." She pointed at each of them with a flash of anger. "I know you guys helped me out, I'll be forever grateful for that, but I don't just need a ride to Texas. I need help. I need help dealing with the murder of my boss, Dr. Blackstone; such a nice, nice man. I need help dealing with a bag full of seeds that could save us, all of us, the whole damn human race. I need help hiding from Blackstone's killers. I need help to keep from getting my ass deported…" she stole a breath. "So, I need the both of you." Blood throbbed behind her eyes, and she straightened her back, knowing she had to say it, knowing she had to get the message across. "I need my friends," she pointed at each of them again then spoke in even steps, a slow trod across the desert: "I can't do this without my friends…"

She leaned against the car, took an uneven breath, and told herself she could keep it together.

"Hey," Keaton spoke softly.

"We'll figure this out," Harry said.

She wiped her eyes with her sleeve. The men both

seemed a little pale, like they'd just given a couple of pints to the Red Cross. A long moment hung in the dry air, then a look crossed from one to the other, a conversation between brothers.

"Harry, uh, she makes some good points." Keaton tapped the hood of the Chevy.

"Yeah, yeah, she does," Harry agreed.

"How about we take you into Colorado," Keaton said to Harry.

"Pot's legal there, you know," Harry raised a brow. "Lower risk."

"That's true, I guess." Keaton cleared his throat. "How about we all get back on the road. Is that OK with you, Lila?"

Her head felt like a fifty-pound helmet had been removed, her neck and shoulders surprisingly flexible again. She hadn't realized how bottled up she'd been about these guys, and her words had left her relieved and clear-headed. She'd said what she had to say. Maybe it would have a lasting effect on them, maybe not. But at least she'd said it, her feelings released.

She nodded, sniffled, and got into the back seat. Harry and Keaton climbed into the front.

They left the parking lot, gassed up the car, and merged onto the highway. Harry and Keaton were not engaged in conversation, but she hoped their silence was not meant to be confrontational, at least for a while. Sunlight glared through the windows, shadows sharp and deep, until the Chevy dipped behind the prairie hills. Tires spun at sixty-five miles an hour across the macadam, louder than in modern cars, and the rhythm tugged her eyelids low.

She adjusted the cooler on the floor, loosened her seat belt, and stretched out across the back seat. The ceiling rocked gently with the road and passing cars, lights and shadows fleeting across the metal roof top in waves. Though it was daylight, she was exhausted and soon sound asleep, dreaming about giant chokecherry bushes and pistols firing into the night.

CHAPTER 29

When the rocking stopped, she woke and rubbed her eyes. A faint smell of petroleum wafted through the vehicle. She climbed from the car, awkward from sleepiness, and found her way to the gas station restroom. When she returned, Harry had taken the wheel. She took a long drink of water then fell into another restless sleep.

When she woke again, the sky had dimmed, and it seemed like she'd never been asleep at all. She sat up and tried to gather her senses. Harry was still driving but they were off the interstate in a town of some sort. He pulled the car into a parking lot and turned off the engine.

"Found a thrift shop for you." He pointed at a building with a tall cross.

"Oh, yes." She took some cash from her daypack and slid from the car. Twenty minutes later, she tossed a bag of clothes through the open car door and followed it inside.

"We decided to get a hotel room here so everyone can get cleaned up and get a nap. We'll pay for the room, get two beds and a roll-away. Then maybe hit the road again tonight," Harry said.

She was relieved there was still some sort of truce between them.

"OK with you?" Keaton asked.

Share a room with these guys? She'd certainly trusted them a lot already, after all. And she sure as hell needed a hot shower and change of clothes. "Deal."

They drove a short way toward the edge of town and pulled into a motel called the Tumble Inn, a neon oak tree watching over visitors at the porte cochère.

Hot water pounded the stress from her shoulders and a fresh pair of jeans and checkered shirt buoyed her spirits. She brushed the knots from her wet hair then sat on the edge of one of the beds.

Keaton took his turn in the shower.

Harry sat in a chair by the front door, phone in hand. "I talked with Keaton about this and, after some thought, I've decided I need to call Johnny."

"Oh?"

"I think those goons of his, Cole and Meatball, are acting on their own, trying to steal what I promised to deliver. They're morons, yes, but dangerous ones. I need to let Johnny know he's being double-crossed by his own guys." Harry loosened the hair in his ponytail.

"Will that keep them from trying again?" Lila asked.

"I don't think so, but Johnny can warn the guy I'm delivering to. Forewarned is forearmed. And maybe we change the delivery day and location, so those guys won't know how to find us."

"Makes sense, I guess."

"I think it's the best we can do," Harry nodded.

"So, they know the current delivery place? And who you are delivering it to?" she asked.

"Unfortunately, I'm sure they do."

"Yes. Speaking of which…" She raised her finger in the air.

Harry leaned forward.

"I didn't find a phone number for Frances Knox when we were at the library, before we got so rudely interrupted. I think I should try again. She needs to know that Dr. Blackstone was killed and that we're bringing some chokecherry seeds to her." Lila pulled her phone from her daypack.

"Well…" Harry rubbed his chin.

"You don't think I should?"

"Don't know for sure. But I guess your boss trusted her," he said.

"He wanted me to mail the seeds to her. If someone killed Blackstone to get them, they might know about her, too. I at least need to warn her."

"Right."

She logged onto the internet and searched again for a phone number for F. Knox in Fabens, Texas. After a few moments, she found one that matched the address she'd found in the library.

Harry punched Johnny's number into his phone and Lila decided to give him some privacy. She left the room and walked around the parking lot, passing by the blue Bel Air. A woman and two children rolled suitcases behind them and loaded them into a silver minivan. An elderly couple climbed into a Lexus with Colorado plates and drove away from the lot. A man in a red pickup stared into a phone in his hands.

She called and heard a beep, then a pleasant female voice insisting that the caller leave a message. Lila introduced herself and said that she was on her way to Knox to deliver seeds at Blackstone's request. She couldn't bring herself to leave the news of Blackstone's murder on a voicemail. She'd try again later.

A cool breeze chilled the wet hair on her head, so she tucked the phone into her pocket and moved back toward the hotel room to warm up.

****

Knox set her phone back into her desk. Streaks of gray blended from her roots into blonde-dyed hair cut just above the shoulders. Pale eyes peeked from behind her wrinkled lids, lines creasing past her lips, converging in loosened flesh below her chin.

Damn fool Blackstone, she thought. He'd never

gotten over his boyish crush on her and now he'd done something really, really stupid. Some college girl had what must be the seeds Blackstone had left his messages about. Seeds that could change Knox's life. Seeds that could change the world. Seeds that could get them all killed if they didn't have an ally, someone else to deal with the repercussions.

"Damn it," she spoke into empty air.

CHAPTER 30

They pulled the motel curtains closed, hung the "do not disturb" sign on the handle, and slept through the night.

Lila woke early and hungry and longing for a hot cup of coffee. Harry stirred slowly, but Keaton was up like a jackrabbit, taking another shower. Lila washed a breakfast bar down with a cup of water and peeked outside at the parking lot.

Not much going on there.

When the guys were ready, the three of them walked across the street to one of those restaurants that served breakfast 24 hours a day. She finished two eggs over easy, three link sausages, and part of a two-stack of buttermilk pancakes. They each took a cup of coffee to go.

They used the motel restroom again, then Keaton went to the car to toss in their gear. Harry went to the front office to check out. Lila stood outside the room and stretched her arms and back. Sunlight bleached the sky to a faint, watery blue. The pickup she'd seen last night was gone.

When Harry left the office, Lila crossed the lot to join him at the car.

Keaton was pulling something from a row of thick bushes about fifty feet away. "Chokecherries!" he announced, cradling berries in his upturned shirt. "Ripe." He seemed relaxed, a little more settled than yesterday.

"Oh, yeah," she said, "nice find."

Keaton went to the trunk, rustled around, and came back to the driver's seat. "All set?"

"Yes," she said.

Harry nodded then looked to Lila, a question in his eyes.

Keaton consulted the paper map. "We're less than two hours from Colorado Springs, on route 24, so this is where we start to dip south."

"We'll all go together, today? A little farther?" Lila's words seemed to tip-toe off her tongue, eager to scurry back to safety in case her question should be withdrawn.

"I've got an old acquaintance west of Walsenburg who might put us up for a couple of nights," Keaton said.

"Yes?" she leaned forward.

"It would save us all some money on hotels." Keaton looked at Harry, who seemed glued into place. "And I'm sure it's a safe place for the drugs…"

Harry winced.

"… and it'll give us time to decide what to do next."

Was their truce beginning to crack? What was Keaton going to do about Harry and the bags of marijuana? Leave him and the pot with this acquaintance of his?

"I'll call him to see if he'll put us up for a night or two. We might get there in about seven hours, not counting a couple of stops and considering we're not exactly speeding in the Bel Air."

"We haven't seen anyone following us lately," Harry said.

"So far." Keaton raised a brow.

"So far, so good," Lila added from the back seat, patting them each on the shoulder, wishing Keaton would relent.

They drove for a while, then Keaton told them about Neville King, the military support contractor he'd met after Harry's brother had been killed in Afghanistan. Keaton explained that Neville had been a jack-of-all-trades, a guy who could rewire a helicopter panel, repair an alternator, or find the right part for your jeep on the black market. Like a bunch of other guys, he and Keaton had swapped stories over off-duty beers in the compound. Born in Manchester, England, Neville had moved to Indianapolis as a boy. They used to reminisce about short skirts in White River Park, bemoan the luck of the Colts, and gossip about racers at the Indy 500. Neville had retired eight years ago and moved to a remote spot near Chucaro, Colorado.

Keaton called Neville, who immediately agreed to

let them stay with him.

They drove south to Walensburg on Interstate 25, the streaming traffic humming like a tunnel of angry bees. Then the old Chevy took them southwest on routes 160 and 12, where the pace of life relaxed. Pines covered rough, low mountains like a rag wool blanket, loose fibers twisting toward the sky.

Keaton had gotten instructions from Neville the old-fashioned way – by asking. When Lila tried to find the cabin on the internet, she found conflicting directions to places that may or may not have been the right target, then lost any connection to the cell towers entirely.

They turned right onto a stony road that wound through thick forest, an open meadow, then more forest, the gravel on the drive eventually dissipating into dusty washboard and shallow ruts.

The lane made a tight curve to their left and opened to a level field of sagebrush and grass, a sunny spot drilled into a sea of darkened pines. They rode slowly toward a fork in the driveway, a wooden garage or barn to their left, a modern cabin to their right. A white pickup truck sat near the porch. They drove to a parking spot near the front of the house and stopped, fresh silence relaxing Lila's shoulders. Heat radiated from the old engine, cooling with its familiar tick-tick-tick.

A man walked around the corner of the barn, rag in hand, and waved. He seemed a little younger than Keaton, reddish face clean-shaven, a bristle-brush of gray covering his head. His shoulders and hips were the same width, the shape of a tube with a slight paunch in its middle.

"Oi!"

Keaton slid out of the Bel Air and the two men shook hands, patting each other on the back, chatting greetings, grins, and nods all around. Keaton introduced Lila and Harry and waved at them to gather their things and follow him and Neville into the house.

The cabin had a modern rustic feel, the wall behind them a naked log like the exterior. The wall to their right was a beige-painted plaster with framed photos of snowy mountains, wide beaches, russet canyons. Farther down, a deer's head with antlers stared into the living room, dead, glassy eyes aimed into the distance. A stuffed magpie hung beyond the deer, it's white-tipped wings spread against the wall as if in flight.

They stood in the front room, picture window behind them. A small kitchen lined the wall to their left: a two-burner range, narrow refrigerator, microwave, and sink. An iron wood stove sat on squat feet by a small window. A large wooden table on narrow legs stood near the stove. Straight ahead was a worn leather couch and, behind that, a room with an open door. An antique wooden rack held three rifles upright. To the right of that was a smaller room with a carved outhouse affixed to the entry, no doubt the bathroom. Next to that, a passage led to the backdoor.

Off her right shoulder was another room, maybe the main bedroom. A smaller room lay beyond that and then a doorway between there and the back wall, maybe for a small closet or a basement.

"Why don't you put that car of yours in my garage?" Neville offered. "It's unlocked."

"Give me the keys, Keaton, and I'll move it," Harry held out his hand.

Keaton tossed him the keys and Harry went outside again.

"I'll get us a cuppa tea." Neville went to the small kitchen. "Tell me, what brings you to see me after all these years? How long's it been?"

"I'd need a calculator." Keaton laughed and sat on the couch.

"Me, too." He placed a kettle onto the burner.

"We really appreciate a place to stay tonight, Nev."

"No problem, ol' mucker."

"We've had some problems on the way…" Keaton laced his fingers together. "We have a delivery down near El Paso and a couple of gorillas have been following us."

"Following you?"

Lila sat across from the couch.

"In my experience, people following you want one of three things." Neville pulled four mugs from a cabinet and turned toward them. "To gather intel, to steal something from you, or to kill you."

"Oh," Keaton glanced at Lila. "I guess…"

"So, which is it?" Neville placed a tea bag into each of the mugs.

"They want something of Harry's."

"I see." The kettle began to whistle, and Neville turned off the burner. "Must be something pretty valuable, but..." he raised the palm of his hand, "don't tell me – it's not my bloody business, you know."

"Well, it is sitting in your garage overnight," Keaton said.

"Not that old bucket of bolts?" Neville poured water into each of the mugs.

"Hey, that's an antique Chevy there," Keaton feigned a zealous defense.

"Oh, OK," Neville patted the air. "I forgot what a classic car guy you were."

"And, no, it's not the Chevy."

Neville handed Keaton and Lila their tea.

"Just something in the trunk, is all," Keaton mumbled.

Was he going to tell his friend what it was? How could he be angry with Harry for hiding the same thing?

Neville rose a brow. "I'll put a bolt on the garage latch tonight, if it'll make you feel better."

"Thanks."

"Not to pry, buddy, but should we expect unwanted guests tonight?"

Surely, Neville had a notion that what was in the trunk was something fishy – contraband, high value, maybe both. Keaton had just alerted him to that much, at least.

She stared at Keaton, her focus packed with accusation and judgment: this is what Harry did to you.

Keaton's line of sight met hers and he flinched, infinitesimally, a quick confusion fleeting across his face. He seemed to shake it loose and returned his gaze to Neville. "I'm sure we've lost them, Nev, or we wouldn't have come here. Really."

"No, of course, my friend. No worries anyway. I've got cameras and alarms all over the house and garage, so if there's any funny business, we'll have good warning. And you know me…"

Keaton canted his head.

"…I'm nothing if not well armed." He reached for the other two mugs.

Harry came back inside and handed the keys to Keaton.

Neville handed a cup of tea to Harry. "I was just telling Keaton I'll lock up the garage tonight."

"Cool." Harry sat on the couch.

Neville pulled a chair from the kitchen table and sat across from them. "We take security seriously here on the King ranch." He smiled and lifted the mug to his lips. He tossed a sly glance at Lila.

CHAPTER 31

Lila tucked a loose hair behind her ear. "I hate to be a bother, but I sure could use a hot shower."

"Where are my manners?" Neville put his tea on the table. "That's the guest bedroom." He pointed. "Next to that, the guest bathroom. Clean towels already there, and soap and shampoo on the sink."

Lila stood. "Thank you. I'll need to get in the back seat for clean clothes."

Harry nodded. "It's open – only the trunk is locked."

"There's one king size bed in the room, big enough for two, and the couch is pretty comfortable," Neville said.

"Harry and I will take the room, then," Keaton took another sip of tea.

"Perfect," Neville agreed.

Lila left her daypack at Harry's feet, casting him a quick "keep an eye on this" glance, and went outside to the garage. The door hung from a metal bar with rollers, so she slid it open. Inside, the walls were paneled in faux walnut sheets, something built in the 1970s. A workbench lined the back wall. The Chevy sat on oil-stained concrete, the floor along the right wall made of dusty plywood. She gathered just what she needed from the thrift store bag on the rear seat and went back into the log house.

Keaton and Neville were discussing their time in Afghanistan, Harry listening intently. Though Neville was not in the military, his company provided logistical support for the troops and got to know many of them in the process. It sounded like Neville had become something of an entrepreneur in his time there, connecting with residents, providing them, and the troops, with supplies not readily available through official channels. Neville bragged a bit about skirting regulations, no doubt exaggerating the tale. Though it all seemed in good humor, Keaton stiffened just a bit at some of it.

Lila luxuriated in the hot water until a twinge of guilt crept in – she needed to save some for the guys. She toweled and brushed her hair then dressed in clean clothes and opened the door to let the steam escape.

Neville and Keaton had set the table and they all enjoyed fresh beef stew, slow cooked in Neville's crock pot, and a bottled local brew. The sun set quickly this deep in the woods, and the day seemed much later than it was. She half-listened to Neville chatter on, his speech a midwestern accent peppered with the odd British uptick at the end of his words. Harry and Keaton took turns in the shower while Neville went to secure the garage and, as he put it, "have a gander at the grounds." He said he'd lock the Chevy for them.

They sat politely in the living room for another while, then Harry stretched and yawned and said it was past his bedtime. Neville handed Lila a sheet, pillow, and blankets for the couch and the men went to their respective rooms. She prepared the couch and looked in the kitchen for a glass for water, which she set on a table by one of the living room chairs. She had no evening clothes, so she loosened the belt on her cotton pants for more comfort sleeping. She turned off all the lights except a small one over the kitchen range. Heat radiated from the old wood stove with a faint scent of iron. She tugged her socks off, dropping them onto the hardwood floor by her pack.

She was relieved to finally rest and fell quickly into a heavy sleep.

Lila woke much later, it seemed, to the sound of the wooden floor creaking under someone's step. Probably Harry or Keaton treading to the bathroom. The sound moved slowly closer, and she imagined Keaton checking on her, the thought itself a comfort. A shoe slid under the edge of the couch.

She lay still, listening, feeling cozy and safe.

Then she felt a man's breath hot against her face, the stale scent of a musty pub jarring her thoughts.

CHAPTER 32

She kept her breaths deep and regular despite the un-comfortable feeling engendered by someone so close to her when she was, apparently, sleeping. Then the odor of stale beer left as quickly as it had arrived, and the man's feet stepped quietly away.

She took a deeper breath and opened one eye.

The man tread slowly down the hallway, beyond, she guessed, the guest bedroom. A hinge released two quick squeaks as it opened and closed again. Steps be-came muffled as the sound faded into silence.

She raised herself on one elbow and peered over the back of the couch. The door by the rear exit was slightly ajar, a dim light silhouetting its shape. The door to the guest bedroom was shut all the way – whoever it was had not gone there.

She sat upright, tightened her belt, and pulled on her socks. She stood slowly, listening intently for any sounds in the house.

All was quiet.

She slid her feet slowly across the floor, moving toward the open door. She pulled the handle back a bit, light flowing over her from below.

The door opened to a set of stairs that descended into a basement.

Was Neville down there? Why had he watched her so closely?

She pulled the door past the quick squeak and listened for any response.

No sound rose from below.

Should she go down the steps? If she ran into Neville, she'd tell him she'd heard someone downstairs and was just checking. Right?

Why was whatever he did in the middle of the night any of her business? Maybe he was an insomniac with a workshop in the cellar…

But the light below was too dim to use for reading or tinkering. She put her foot onto the first step and shifted her weight onto it. The stair was solid and silent.

She took another step down, then another, and lowered herself to peek into the basement below. The walls were barren cinder blocks, the floor an ashen concrete. An old washer and dryer sat next to each other at the bottom of the stairs. Boxes and a cluttered table rested against the far wall.

Where the hell was he?

Weak light filtered through something on the wall beneath the steps, drawing her farther down to see. When she reached the floor, she hung onto the railing and turned toward the tepid glow. A sheet of plywood rested against the wall. Next to that was a hole about three feet wide and four feet tall.

The light projected from inside a tunnel.

She stepped carefully along the floor and stopped just outside the entrance. She peered into the hole and stared.

Why was there a tunnel here?

Pine two-by-fours and sheets of plywood shored the sides and ceiling every few feet, bare dirt between the sporadic walls. The earthen floor was well packed, chevrons of dried mud scattered along the surface. A single extension cord snaked its way along the top, draped over crooked nails, to a naked bulb that might be halfway through. The end of the empty tunnel blurred into blackness.

Neville must be down here, but, surely, he was too far away to see or hear her. She bent at the waist and took one tentative step inside, feeling the cold soil through her socks, the chill leaching up her bones. She walked two more steps and then could see the end of the tunnel and a wooden ladder rising to somewhere else.

Where did it lead?

The absence of sound was oppressive. She wanted to stand upright, but when she tried, the roof pushed down against her shoulders. The air pressurized in her lungs, squeezing her breath.

The length was probably only forty yards. Just forty strides to the end. She could get there and back in under a minute.

She really should turn back.

But why would someone put a tunnel here? What secret place lay at the end? Was this some kind of escape into the woods?

She strode quickly now, with purpose, crossing to the light bulb and beyond, when her form suddenly spread a shadow in front of her, all the way to the ladder.

There, she heard sounds from above – metal slamming, boots scraping against the floor. A branch of the tunnel yawned to her right for a yard, then stopped. A work in progress?

She climbed the ladder, light now visible in the room above, sounds as loud as clashing dinner plates, and she peeked above the rim.

The tunnel led to the garage. Why would he need to tunnel here? All he had to do was walk from the cabin across the yard. Unless the garage was just a way station to somewhere else, the tunnel not yet complete...

Neville's back was toward her. He was pulling stuff from the trunk of the Chevy and carefully searching through it.

CHAPTER 33

She could hardly believe what she was seeing. Neville had picked the small lock on one of the bags of Harry's pot – actually, Johnny's pot – and was unrolling the top. He stared inside for a moment then released a slow, low whistle that echoed through the garage.

Was Neville going to alert the police? Should she?

Neville rolled the top closed again and re-fastened the lock.

Lila lowered her head below the opening and took one careful step back down the wooden ladder.

A heavy thunk sounded above her. Neville seemed to be moving gear back into the trunk.

She took another step down.

She could hear shuffling against the concrete floor.

She put her left toes on the bottom rung and, as she shifted her weight onto it, her stocking foot slipped off the two-by-four and onto the ground with a hard beat.

The sounds up by the Chevy stopped.

The root of her tongue thickened, her skin prickling.

Boots skidded against the concrete above her, moved to readiness.

She put her other foot on the ground and began to turn.

Footfalls pounded toward her, an elephant beating toward the edge of the escarpment. She ran from the ladder hunched forward, escape her only thought, and she sped toward the middle of the hand-dug mine, not quite under the bare light bulb that hung from the ceiling, and stopped, looking back over her shoulder, searching for any sign that Neville was coming after her.

An eerie silence suffocated the earthen passage.

She noticed her own shadow, stretching toward the ladder, yet, thankfully, just short of it, just beyond the view of anyone searching from above.

She tried to keep her breaths slow and quiet, staring at the ladder until her eyes began to sting.

A low, scraping sound reached the depths of the tunnel.

Was he coming down? Her muscles tensed.

Or had he turned away?

Moments blended into minutes as the scratching noises faded and she finally concluded he'd returned to the car.

She moved steadily under the bare light bulb, then past it, her shadow now leading the way back toward the musty basement.

When she reached the exit, she ducked behind the cellar wall and watched inside the tunnel, making sure that Neville was not following. Was he circling back above ground - crossing the yard to come to the cabin through the front door?

She hurried to the staircase and climbed to the top, panting a bit for air. She closed the door, past the squeak in the hinges, to where it was positioned when she'd first found it.

What was Neville's reason for searching the Chevy? Keaton had told him they had something that someone was chasing them to steal. Did Neville distrust Keaton? Now he knew that marijuana was in the green dry bags. Would Neville call the police? Wasn't weed legal in Colorado now? Or was it legal only for licensed growers? Legal or not, had Neville decided to steal it for himself?

Click. A door around the corner had just closed. Had Neville returned? Had Harry or Keaton been up a moment ago? Had they noticed she was not on the couch?

She waited, listening intently. Whoever it was must have used the toilet and gone back to bed. She shuffled quietly across the hall. The restroom light was out, so she slid inside. She used the bathroom quickly then climbed back onto the couch and covered herself with blankets, arranging them as best she could to match what she'd done earlier. Slowly, heat began to return to her frigid toes and her breathing relaxed. She waited to hear Neville's return but finally fell into a fitful slumber, trying to push the damp, dirt tunnel away from her dreams, but without success.

CHAPTER 34

Lila awoke to the clang and scrape of pots and plates in the kitchen and the compelling smell of hot coffee and frying bacon. Still, she feigned sleep, not wanting to be alone with Neville.

When she heard Keaton ask Neville for sugar and cream, she pulled the blankets to her neck and opened her eyes. A tawny glow radiated outside the front room window, warming the lodge pole pine.

"Good morning, sleepy head." Neville's honeyed voice was a bit too intimate for comfort. Or was she imagining it?

She slid her feet to the floor. "Morning." The bathroom was empty, so she hurried in and closed the door. She readied for the day, brushing her dark hair to a sheen, straightening her thrift store shirt, checking the mirror. Procrastinating. Harry's laughter filtered under the door. She forced herself to finish.

THE ANTIDOTE

"There she is," Harry smiled. "Coffee?"

"Of course." She sat at the small table between Harry and Keaton.

"Feeling OK today?" Keaton asked of everyone.

She nodded.

"Carpe diem." Harry raised his mug in the air in a toast to the day.

Neville placed before her a plate of scrambled eggs, bacon, and a cinnamon roll.

"Thank you," she said, a cheer in her voice she didn't feel.

Neville's eyes, depthless as river stones, watched her face, then moved away, betraying nothing. He patted Harry's shoulder and moved back to the stove for more food.

She tore into her food with renewed purpose: to fill her empty belly and avoid Neville's polished eyes for as long she possibly could.

Keaton compared their old army food to Neville's, the two chuckling at references to people and places she knew nothing about, but then the men went quiet, hunger taking charge of their ambition. She finished her eggs and took a sip of coffee with each taste of her roll, working herself up to ask a question.

"What's the plan for today, guys?" She lifted the coffee to her lips, partially shielding her face.

"You should spend the day here." Neville's lips smiled, a thin warmth. "Take a break from your travels and rest up."

163

"Nice offer," Keaton replied.

She spit a bit of coffee back into the mug.

"Steak dinner tonight." Neville nodded toward the kitchen range. "Wine for the lady," he glanced at Lila, "beer for the grunts."

Hell, no. She did her best not to grimace.

Harry seemed suddenly constipated. "We should get back on the road, though…"

Keaton rubbed his chin.

"Well, at least stay for a solid meal," Neville looked to Keaton. "Can't turn down a free steak, can you?"

Keaton glanced from Neville to Harry to Lila. "I suppose we can hang around for another meal, huh, guys?"

"It's settled then," Neville said. "We'll eat this afternoon then you can get going again before dark."

She kept her eyes on her cinnamon bun as if it was ready to make an escape.

The men finished eating and Harry began clearing the table, stacking dishes in the sink. Neville stood and helped with the clean-up.

When Keaton stood, she saw an opportunity. She swallowed more coffee, now tepid and a little stale, and pushed away from the table.

Keaton stretched and wandered toward the picture window in the living room. Lila rose and joined him.

"How about a walk in the woods? Before it gets too hot out?" she asked.

"Great idea. Hey, Neville, we're going for a walk, OK?"

"'Course. There's a trail out back takes you out aways then loops to the back of the garage."

Harry turned to them. "Your turn for dishes at dinner."

"Always on KP," Neville added, wiping an iron skillet.

Keaton and Lila turned and walked past the guest bathroom, the dead deer and magpie, the cellar door on their right, and through the back exit. Once outside, she took a deep breath and shivered a bit in the morning air.

"Cold?" Keaton asked.

"I'll be fine, just need to get moving." She found the wide path and Keaton moved beside her.

"I have to tell you something, Keaton," she began. "Away from…"

"Hey, wait up ol' mucker," Neville's voice cut through the air. "I put Harry to the hard labor, so I could join you."

"Sure." Keaton waved Neville forward, the three of them on the trail side by side. "What were you saying?" he asked Lila.

This Neville guy was creeping her out and pissing her off at the same time. She looked farther down the path and waved her hand at the pines, thinking of something to say. "Did you know that certain fungus in the earth create pathways between the trees? Underground?"

"No," Keaton said.

Neville seemed to focus on his boots as they walked along.

"Yeah, it's fascinating. Mushrooms are just the tops, the fruit. The rest of the organism can be very large and connect the roots of trees like a web."

"Really?" Keaton looked into the woods. The path narrowed here, and Neville fell in behind them.

"Yeah. There's evidence trees cooperate with each other and these fungi help facilitate that."

"What?"

"Research has shown a parent tree surrendering moisture and even nutrients to its nearby seedlings, to ensure they survive their early years."

"Remarkable." Neville's Manchester accent seemed unnaturally heightened.

Keaton clasped his hands behind his back. "Nothing like a walk in the woods with a botanist, huh?" He smiled at Neville.

"Indeed."

"Makes me think of our old cook Harp. Remember him? Always putting weeds into our food and calling them herbs…"

"Ol' Carp we used to call him," Neville said.

"That's him," Keaton replied, and the men were off again into talk of sergeants and gunners and rations that meant little to Lila. Keaton shifted so he could walk next to Neville and she moved a few yards ahead, wandering through the pines, clusters of greenish Tricholoma, a patch of Boletus mushrooms, and her own lonely thoughts.

If Neville had heard something last night, he wouldn't know it was her. Would he? Was Neville going to forever monopolize conversations with Keaton? Was he doing it so she couldn't talk with Keaton? Maybe she should tell Harry what happened, instead. After all, Neville may be Keaton's old pal but the pot he'd found was Harry's. Or Johnny's. Or someone's.

Hauling over a hundred thousand dollars' worth of marijuana in the trunk of the car was a serious, serious problem. And as much as she liked Harry and Keaton, the problem was raising its ugly head again and again. In fact, it was directly impeding her mission from Dr. Blackstone – getting those chokecherry seeds to Knox. Doesn't she have more important things to do than get caught up in an illicit delivery of Cannabis sativa? And now that Neville knows, what's he going to do? Will he steal it? She had half a mind to help him... Or has he stolen it already?

They had to get back on the road. She couldn't even hitch another ride from here. Nor could she try another call to Knox – there was no cell phone service at Neville's cabin.

The thought of staying a second night here made her shiver.

The trail curved gently back on itself and they

found themselves behind the barn-shaped garage, headed for the cabin again. She moved past the back door to the garage, examining the ground between the buildings for a moment, imagining the tunnel underneath.

She really needed to make a decision. But...

"Hey, Lila, can you help me take a look at my vegetable garden a moment?" Neville asked. "I could really use a botanist's help with my tomatoes next year – I don't know why my crop keeps getting smaller and smaller."

Hell, no. "Sure." She glanced behind at the men. "Just let me use your bathroom first." She pointed and moved ahead, not waiting for more discussion.

She reached the cabin, hurried into the restroom, and waited. Keaton and Neville passed by outside, chatting again about grunts, K-rations, names of men she knew nothing about. Their voices moved out of range.

She opened the door and peeked out. Across the hall was the display of hunting rifles, the apathetic deer head, the stuffed magpie. The men were all seated on the front porch, backs to the cabin. The bathroom was almost directly across from the small room next to the doorway to the cellar. What was in that narrow room? Storage? Another passageway?

She dried her hands on a towel and moved to the doorway across the hall. She stood there, watching the men gesture with hands and arms, voices muffled through the glass. She leaned forward, touching the handle, then turned it slowly.

Click.

The men continued talking.

She quickly slid inside the room and searched for a light. An array of four twelve-inch monitors lined a table against the side wall, powerless and blank. A central computer and keyboard rested near the edge of the table-top by a swivel chair. Wires ran from the monitors up the walls and disappeared into the ceiling. The monitors were labeled: "front," "garage outer," "rear," and... "tunnel."

CHAPTER 35

Voices outside the cabin grew louder. She closed the door to the computer room and stepped quickly to the back side of the couch.

Neville gave a quick wave to Keaton and Harry and looked into the house for a moment, searching behind the glare of the picture window. Then he turned and stepped off the porch, striding purposefully toward the white pickup truck parked by the cabin.

Harry and Keaton shuffled inside, closing the front door behind them.

"There she is," Harry smiled.

Lila moved to the window, joints stiff with tension.

Neville climbed into the truck and pulled away, bouncing down the dirt road, through the grassy flat, and into the forest.

"Where's he going?" she asked.

"Into town for steaks and beer. And wine for you."

Harry pointed at the window behind him. "For the cook-out."

"Cook-out?" the words burst from her mouth.

Harry's lips tightened. "You OK?"

"No, Harry, none of us are." She waved at them to sit on the couch, but she remained standing, pacing before them, glancing out the window.

"What?" Keaton sat tentatively, ready to jolt upright in case the furniture was electrified.

"I have to tell you guys something." She drew a breath.

"What's wrong?" Harry asked.

"I woke up last night and Neville was standing over me, breathing on my face, so I pretended to be asleep. It was really creepy, so I listened, and I heard him go down steps, back there." She pointed at the doorway to the basement.

"I waited a while then followed him downstairs and I found something...a tunnel. A tunnel that goes to the garage."

"Neville's always been a little paranoid, you know," Keaton explained, "preparing for the apocalypse—"

"No, well yes." She wrung her fingers, eyes on the floor. "I went into the tunnel and there's a ladder at the end, and I went up it and I found Neville there, searching through all our stuff."

"What?" Harry sat upright.

"Yeah, he had it all laid out on the floor, and he

picked a lock on one of those green dry bags, the ones with the marijuana in them, and he opened it and found what was inside."

Keaton's face twisted in confusion.

"Shit." Harry stood up.

"Yeah, he broke into the trunk and had it all spread out like he was…doing an inventory or something."

"I can't believe he'd do that." Keaton squinted, disbelief and accusation in his words.

"We should go and look," Harry said.

She glanced out the window. The white truck was nowhere to be seen.

"He'll be nearly an hour." Harry nodded toward the driveway outside. "It takes a while to get to the highway, where there's a little store."

"Then let's go now." Lila hurried around the furniture and past the cadaverous deer. "In there's his computer room, with monitors." She pointed.

She heard the door open as Harry and Keaton peeked inside.

She moved to the cellar door, opening it past the squeak in the dry hinge, starting down the steps. Keaton and Harry's boots clomped behind her.

A piece of plywood covered part of the tunnel entrance. She slid it aside and it fell from her hands to the floor, banging, kicking up dust.

"Holy…" Harry said at the tunnel entrance.

Keaton's dark eyes seemed to fill with worry.

She ducked her head and led them inside. The light was off, and she'd forgotten to look for a switch, so she felt along the walls as she went, ambient light from the cellar dimming as she went. Her hands suddenly felt the wooden ladder. Light crept through tiny fissures in the roof above.

She stepped up the ladder and felt along the top. Two handles attached to a stout piece of plywood. She pushed them up, raising the lid, and sunlight glowed deeper into the tunnel. She shoved the board aside, climbed onto the floor of the garage, and stood.

Harry and Keaton followed her.

The Chevy sat where Harry had parked it the day before. The floor lay empty, none of their things in sight.

"Let's check the trunk." She dusted off her pants.

Harry strode to the back of the car and felt below the trunk, running his fingers along the edge, pushing and twisting the mechanism.

"You'll need the key." Keaton offered it to Harry.

Suddenly, the trunk popped open.

"It shouldn't do that without this." Keaton raised the key chain in the air.

"The latch's been bent out of shape," Harry said.

"He broke into it." Lila moved closer to the car.

"He's messed up the lock," Harry said, moving behind her.

Keaton raised the hood.

Inside, the contents seemed as if they'd never been

touched. "He's put them all back where they were when he started," Lila said.

"He got into the dry bags, right?" Harry asked.

She nodded. "He whistled when he looked inside one of them."

Harry leaned past her and pulled out one of the green bags. He placed it on the floor, upright, and they examined it.

"This has been opened," Harry pointed. "The way this has been wound shut, it's got one less roll in it. See…" His finger slid over the rubberized material. It's looser here. There's more space, more air on the top than when Johnny closed it."

"You don't have a key, do you?" Lila asked.

"I do, for emergencies.

"I think this qualifies," she said.

"Let's see if he messed with what's inside." Harry pulled a tiny key from his jeans, unlocked the top, and unrolled the bag. Inside was another bag, tied in a loose knot. He picked at it until the plastic slid the rest of the way free and he pulled it clear.

They each peered inside.

The pot was still there, in tight, green clumps, the scent like sweetened hay.

"Why would he work so hard to keep his, his… break-in, so hidden…?" Lila asked.

"…and not steal the weed?" Harry finished her question.

They stood there a moment, flummoxed.

"Shit," Lila put her hand to her head. "He didn't want the pot. He isn't after the pot."

"Could he have just wanted to find out what we were hiding?" Harry said.

"All that effort to satisfy a little curiosity?" Lila asked, her voice heavy with skepticism.

"Or...he already knew about Blackstone's seeds and that's what he's really after." Keaton's words echoed through the garage, chilling her lungs.

CHAPTER 36

"But how can that be?" Lila stared at the marijuana.

"Bastard." Keaton pronounced it like a simple, maddening fact, his brow lowered, his nose flared, a reaction to the rotting truth.

"Right. How did he know about Blackstone's seeds?" Harry asked.

The weight of the question bogged them down, their thoughts struggling to run through waist-high waters. Keaton's dark eyes relaxed into the distance, to that place where ideas hide. Harry put his hands on the sides of his head and flexed, a momentary display of trauma.

She pulled a deep breath. "Whoever is after us, they've got some serious money. They've been searching all over, knowing we're trying to get to Knox with the seeds, trying to intercept us. They've got friends out there looking for us. Anyone and everyone they know, and everyone they know, are all on the look-out or waiting around the corner."

"Neville wanted us to stay for dinner; to stay another night." Keaton had returned from his mental outpost.

"He's got reinforcements on the way." Lila put her fists on her hips.

"Whoever they are, they do have a lot of help." Keaton nodded. "A lot more than just those two who've been hot on our tail."

"They'd have to be paying people some serious shit." Harry shook his head in disgust.

"And more than what that pot is worth," she said.

"Indeed." The faintly British accent shattered the room like broken glass. "Although, there's really no reason not to take both of them." Neville rose from behind the car, black pistol aimed at the ceiling.

Her heart seemed to stop mid-beat, life-giving oxygen sucked from the room.

"I thought you went to the market," Keaton accused, clenching his fists.

"No, no. I checked my camera feeds late last night. I knew that Lila, here," he pointed with the pistol, "would tell you about me finding your precious marijuana. So, I went 'round the bend and parked. Hurried through the back door just as you were coming out of the tunnel." He stepped around the grill of the Chevy and faced them head-on.

"You were looking for Blackstone's seeds and you found the pot?" she asked.

"Right-o."

"How…?" Keaton asked.

"An acquaintance from my old company called me. It's a small world in the military contract business, ol' mucker, seven degrees of separation and all that rot. Said there were six figures in it for me if I had information leading his client to you or to these seeds of yours. Imagine his surprise when I told him I'd already heard from you. That you were on your way to my cabin."

Keaton's cheeks and forehead flushed.

She took a step forward. Harry reached his arm in front of her.

"When you said you had something special in your trunk," he motioned toward the Chevy, "I assumed it was those seeds. But I found two bags of high-grade marijuana instead."

Neville slid toward the workbench behind him.

"Which means," he continued, "that you still have the seeds, somewhere else. Maybe hidden in the car, maybe in your suitcase or bags, maybe in Lila's day pack."

Her stomach wrung like rags in a knot. "Are you going to kill us?" She heard her own voice squeak through her teeth, a disembodied plea.

"No need for that. I'm holding you here until, as you guys in the army like to say, the cavalry arrives. They'll find those seeds, pay me my fee, and be on their way."

"Do you have any idea what those seeds can do?" she asked.

"Don't know. Don't care."

Keaton took two steps forward.

Neville raised the pistol, his lips clamped with determination.

Harry moved next to Keaton and touched his arm, urging him to stay.

"And the pot?" Lila asked.

"Yes, there's no need for my friends to know about that. Think of it as my tip for the fine service I've provided." He reached behind him and pulled a roll of twine from the work bench. "Harry, slide those dry bags over to me, will you? Lila, you're going to tie up Keaton's hands, behind his back." He tossed the roll of heavy string into the air.

Lila followed the arc of the twine, then watched Harry heave a dry bag toward Neville, Keaton rushing behind it.

The twine bounced to a stop on the floor.

Keaton plowed into Neville behind the bag, shoving him against the workbench with a sudden slam. Neville's fingers fanned open, as wide as his eyes. The pistol clattered into tools, and junk spread across the bench and Neville folded forward, jabbing his elbow into Keaton's back.

Lila stepped forward to help, but Harry grabbed her from behind, holding her away from the fight.

Keaton staggered away. Neville quickly advanced, right shoulder winding back, clenching his fist, then twisting at the waist, punching Keaton hard against his stomach, and she dreaded whether an older man could handle such a beating.

Harry spread his arms, keeping her out of the fray.

Keaton swung a glancing blow against Neville's jaw, but Neville struck again, and Keaton fell to the ground.

Neville moved into position, raising his elbow for another vicious jab into Keaton's back when Harry rushed forward, wrapping an arm below Neville's chin, yanking him backward, and pushing his free hand into the base of Neville's neck. Neville whirled his arms vainly in the air, uttering deep and desperate grunts of resistance, a wild pig in distress. Then, Neville dropped under Harry's weight, all of his brutish menace suddenly and definitively unplugged.

CHAPTER 37

Lila rested her hands on her knees, bent and breathing hard, watching Neville as he lay on the concrete floor. Harry stood and turned to her.

"Tie up this piece of shit, would you?"

She nodded, trying to process what she'd seen. Keaton was on all fours, head down, lungs heaving. Harry went to him, telling him he was all right, rubbing his back.

She searched for the roll of twine and unrolled a length of it. She stepped close to Neville, who had collapsed. Cautiously, she pulled one of his arms into position, then the other, and began to tie the tough string on one of his wrists.

Keaton grunted as he stood, Harry helping him to balance.

Lila wrapped the twine around the wrist she'd tied then wrapped it, again and again, around the other wrist, and then both, and made her best square knot four times, just to be sure.

Keaton rested against the Chevy and Harry hurried to the workbench. He came to Lila with a pair of wire cutters and worked them over the excess twine until it cut free. Then he pulled Neville straight along the floor, placing his feet together, and bound them tightly.

Lila stared into Neville's slackened face, his eyes closed, drool dripping into the dusty concrete. She put her hand beneath his nose. Was he breathing? Was he dead? She waited and waited, moving her fingers closer and closer until finally she felt the flow of air against her knuckles.

"Nice work," Keaton said to Harry. He'd turned away from the car, holding his ribs.

"You showed me that hold, remember? Push hard on the artery in the neck, as I recall, and you can put a man right under." Harry stood and placed the cutters back onto the workbench.

"Right," Keaton said. "Let's get the hell out of here."

"No argument there," Harry replied.

Lila stood and flung herself into Keaton's chest, hugging him tighter than she should.

"Hey, not so rough there, sister." It was the first time Keaton had used Harry's term – the first time he'd called her that – and she felt some moisture in her eyes.

Harry cleared his throat and went to the trunk. He twisted the bag open and began putting the pot back into it. "Can you run to the cabin and get the rest of our stuff?"

"Of course." Lila pushed away from Keaton, wiping her face with her finger, a little embarrassed, perhaps, but relieved beyond measure.

She asked herself: above ground or below? Above, no question. She went through the back door of the garage and made her way to the rear of the cabin. Inside, she put her pack onto her shoulders and searched the spare bedroom for Keaton's bag and Harry's pack, tossing a loose shirt, comb, and deodorant into the nearest suitcase. When she thought she'd found it all, she carried the luggage to the living room, watching the dead deer glare ahead as she slid out the back door.

She passed Harry outside, on her way to the garage. He waved a pair of bolt cutters at her and said, "The big front door's locked from the outside. Guess he was worried about us leaving in the Chevy."

She frowned at that thought and went through the back door again. Neville still lay on the concrete floor. Keaton was sitting in the passenger seat of the car. She moved straight to the open trunk and placed their gear inside.

The latch on the sliding door jostled and clunked as Harry cut through the lock. He pushed the door open and across its runners, spilling mid-morning light across the Bel Air.

Neville groaned and tightened into a fetal position. Keaton opened the car door and went to Neville, lowering himself to the ground. "Neville, old mucker," his words dripped with sarcasm. "I see you've found yourself in a bit of mess."

Harry waved Lila toward the Chevy. He trotted along the side opposite from Neville and Keaton and slid into the front seat.

Neville's face lifted from the cement; his lips twisted into an angry grin.

Keaton stood and went to the workbench, where he slid the tools away from the edge, as far back toward the wall and away from Neville as he could. "I'm going to leave you right where you are so whoever called you for help can find you, helpless on the floor. If they don't find you, well, you'll find a way out of those ropes eventually, old pal…"

Neville released a low thrumming noise, wasps caught deep in his throat, his cheeks flushing a hearty burgundy.

Lila went to the back door of the Bel Air, resting her hand on the handle, watching Neville twist against his restraints. The engine turned over, and over, and over, then stopped.

A muscle pulsed on Neville's neck. Keaton stepped away from him.

Harry tried again to start the car.

Neville bent at the waist, scooting his legs in front of him, wiggling and then rolling into a seated position.

Lila moved into the back seat of the Chevy, placing

her pack on the floor.

Harry tried a third time to start the car.

"You're not going anywhere, old mucker." Neville smiled now, the grin of Lucifer on his lips, and he pulled his knees to his chest. "I disabled your precious Chevy in case you got the locked garage door open. You will pay dearly for this. My associates will be here soon, and you will pay."

Lila hopped out of the car and went around the back, avoiding Neville. She watched as Keaton hurried to the front of the car and lifted the hood. Inside, he examined wires to mysterious boxes, the generator, and spark plugs. He leaned farther in, pushing each connection to the distributor cap, tugging linkage and fuel lines and hoses.

He withdrew from the engine and moved to the trunk, where he twisted the lock and lifted the cover. Inside, he grabbed his toolbox and trotted back to the engine. He found a screwdriver and released the distributor, examining the parts inside.

"You loosened the points," Keaton said. "You're a bastard, Neville, but not clever enough." He rummaged through his tools, found a gauge of some sort, and inserted it between two small metal plates. He pushed hard on the screwdriver, tightening it in place. He put the cap carefully over the mechanism and clamped it down.

"That's it," he said to Lila.

He closed the hood and followed her to the trunk,

where he returned the toolbox and shoved the lid closed. She went back to the rear door and scooted inside. Keaton got inside the passenger door, pulled it closed, and rolled down his window.

"Try it now," Keaton said to Harry.

The engine rumbled to life.

Neville's cheeks had paled, his eyes now firmly on the floor in front of him.

"Say hi to your friends," Keaton waved.

Harry clunked the Chevy into reverse and darted backward past the garage door, spinning the wheel to his left, skidding tires against the gravel. He straightened as he moved forward but stopped at the fork in the driveway.

"What?" Lila asked.

Harry put the car in park, hopped out, and ran to the white pickup truck. He knelt by the front tire, releasing its air, then to left rear, then he moved to the other side, out of sight. In a moment, he trotted back to the Chevy and slammed it into drive. They roared down the rugged road, sliding, vibrating, bouncing over washboards and ruts until suddenly they reached the smooth asphalt of highway 12 and Lila pulled what felt like the first deep breath she'd ever had.

CHAPTER 38

They sped down highway 12, the Bel Air rocking on her tired shocks, cars whisking past them in the opposite direction, gusts of wind firing through the window wings.

Neither man spoke to the other. Lila looked at Keaton, then Harry, then back at Keaton, trying to make her gestures obvious. Gaining no response, she sat back into the rear seat and huffed, arms folded. How could these guys just sit there, not talking about what had happened back at the cabin? Was Keaton still angry at Harry for the marijuana in his trunk? Hadn't Harry helped Keaton overcome Neville, that little creep? Weren't the two of them better together than apart? Were their male egos really puffed so full of hot air?

They reached Interstate 25 at Trinidad, where Keaton turned south and then off-ramp to a busy truck stop for a break. She pulled the pack onto her shoulders and left the car, acquiescing in their pact of silence.

She used the restroom, washed her face with paper towels, then brushed her hair into a ponytail. She wandered the store with other customers, some eager, some with days of driver's fatigue tugging on their faces. Candy, chips, and Colorado souvenirs lined several rows of shelves, and she walked down each one, watching for Keaton and Harry, staring at packets of peanuts, and thinking about the seeds in her daypack.

Maybe it was time to call the police.

Keaton seemed determined to leave Harry and his pot at a roadside bus somewhere. He'd softened some, and he'd taken them this far, but...

A dark-haired child brushed past her, squealing for her father.

If she called the police, she'd have to duck away from them. Doing that without saying goodbye was out of the question. But she could make a call, arrange to meet with police, and then tell the guys what she'd done. They'd have to agree to leave her off somewhere, a place where the police could pick her up and keep her safe.

USCIS would most likely deport her. Well, maybe she'd just have to face it. Maybe she could complete her studies at McGill University, in Montreal.

If a weirdo like Neville could find her...through Keaton...heading back to Canada alone might be a good idea.

And the longer she stayed with Harry and Keaton, the longer she presented a threat to them. They had enough to worry about – Meatball, she rolled her eyes at the name, and Cole.

Harry was being paranoid about calling the police, but then, he had enough pot in the car to send him to jail for a decade. She'd be paranoid, too. But if she were separated from them, and from the marijuana, wouldn't she be safer?

She searched the store and found Keaton at the check-out stand. Harry lingered by the coffee machine.

Because of its famous Nevada cousin, she remembered the town of Las Vegas, New Mexico, on the map. She could call the police in Las Vegas and get the guys to let her out there. But she'd have to do it quickly.

She tapped on her phone, looking for a phone number. When she found it, she checked on Harry and Keaton again. Keaton had gone outside. Harry was paying for coffee.

She dialed the number. Once the automated system had reminded her to call 911 in emergencies, a female voice picked up the line.

"Vegas police department."

"Hi, I have a question about police protection," she began.

"Name?"

"Let's wait on that for now." She watched Harry turn and circle in front of the register, no doubt looking for her.

"Miss, what can we do for you?"

"I need to know if you can protect me from someone who's trying to catch me."

"Miss, where are you?"

"In...maybe an hour from Las Vegas. I'd like to see a detective there if I can."

"You're not in town?"

"No."

"But you want an appointment?"

"Yes, that's right. With a detective or someone who can protect me."

"Well...why is someone after you? Is this a domestic matter?"

"Domestic? No, no, I've got something he wants, and I need protection against him."

"Is it contraband?"

"Contraband? No."

"But you're not in Las Vegas?"

"But I'll be there soon."

"Do you need directions to the police station?"

"No, I can find those, I just need to explain things to someone in charge, someone who can help. I really just need an appointment for now."

"I'll alert Detective Rogers, but I'll need a name, please."

Harry waved for her to join him.

"I'll call you when I get to town. Detective Rogers. In about an hour."

"Your name, miss?"

Harry walked toward her, two coffees in hand.

"Thank you." She quickly ended the call.

Harry handed her a hot cup and smiled. "Time to go."

She thanked him and followed outside to the Chevy, parked by the station's front glass window, suddenly unsure again whether she should stray from her new-found friends or not.

CHAPTER 39

His partner, Stan, would not tolerate the expense of a chartered jet, so Wormwood hadn't told him. They were well beyond pinching pennies now. He'd already rolled the dice, already bet the last of their business reserves on finding Blackstone's seeds and securing them for Dragon-tree Agri-Economics. He simply had no choice anymore.

His shoes clacked against the terrazzo floor, a steady and determined staccato. A countertop rose to his right. Beside it stood a tired looking woman in her fifties and a stack of pamphlets for local hotels and restaurants.

"Mr. Wormwood?" she asked.

"Yes."

"Your aircraft is ready. It's the Phenom 300, straight out this door." She pointed.

A charter jet was perfect for the task: no waiting in line, no security checks, no metal detectors, no annoying questions. His pistol was in a hard-sided case wrapped inside a towel.

He nodded, briefcase in one hand, duffle in the other. The glass door slid open as he neared, and the sound of a jet engine raked the air.

A man in a white shirt, epaulettes on each shoulder, stood by a set of stairs that unfurled from the plane like an open tongue. Three stripes ran the length of the cream-colored jet, nose to tail.

He acknowledged the pilot, who welcomed him aboard. Inside, he slid the duffle under one of the forward seats and lay his briefcase on a table he swung in front of him. A co-pilot waved at him from the cockpit. The pilot confirmed their destination and estimated flight time, weather conditions, safety protocols. Drinks, snacks, and a restroom were in the rear of the plane.

He'd sample their whiskey once they were in the air.

In a few minutes, the pilot finished his pre-flight procedures and closed a curtain between the passenger compartment and the cockpit.

In moments, they'd lifted from the tarmac and were on their way to Carlsbad, Arizona, the airport closest to the reported route of the girl, the two men, and the seeds. A car awaited him there.

CHAPTER 40

They pulled slowly up the ramp and onto the interstate, trucks and cars passing impatiently until they reached the speed limit. Lila settled into the back seat.

"Listen, Harry and Lila. I've got to say something," Keaton began, eyes on the road ahead. "First, I want to thank the both of you for how you handled yourselves back there with Neville. I thought that guy was a pal."

"The chum turned out to be a chump," Harry said.

"That's it," Keaton agreed, "and I owe you an apology. I trusted Neville and that was a huge mistake. Huge."

"It's OK. Happens to the best of us," Harry said.

"No worries." Lila touched his shoulder.

"No, there's more I need to say." He drew a breath. "When you told me about the marijuana in my trunk, Harry, I blew a gasket. I really did."

Harry stared at the coffee in his hands. "I know."

"And you shouldn't have done that, and you've

promised never to do it again. So, I need to be a big boy
and accept that, and I do."

Harry looked at him.

"I mean, really, Harry, let's not keep anymore shit
from each other, OK? I still think you can't trust Johnny
as far as you can throw him, but after dealing with Neville, well, who am I to judge?"

"Hey, man, it's cool," Harry lifted the coffee, a
one-sided toast to his friend.

Lila leaned forward. "Well, it's about damned
time, you guys. I thought I'd never hear you two speaking to each other again. I'm so very glad to hear this,
guys, really."

"Don't think I'm going to go soft on you." Keaton
pointed at Harry.

"Never would I think such a thing." He grinned.
"Truth is, I'm just too loveable to stay mad at."

Keaton glanced at the ceiling. "Huh."

Harry pointed to himself and Keaton then turned
to Lila. "We've got something a lot more important to do
than stay mad at each other. We've gotta get this young
lady and her magic seeds to a Dr. Knox in Fabens, soon
as we can."

Oh, dear.

"Hey, you guys," she began, wondering just how
to explain herself. Damn it − a single moment of doubt
and she'd taken the wrong track. "I think I made a little
mistake myself."

Keaton looked at her in the rearview mirror. Harry turned sideways in his seat to see her more easily.

"Well, I…" She glanced at each of them then released her thoughts in a rush: "I thought Keaton was going to leave Harry at a bus stop or something. And then I thought maybe I should leave both of you guys, since you'd be separated anyway, not that I wanted to, but if Neville could find me then others might, too, and you guys would be in danger from me as well as from those guys who work for Johnny."

"Oh…" Harry began.

Lila raised her hand, cutting him off. "So, I called the Las Vegas, New Mexico, police to get an appointment with a detective, someone who might be able to help me get safely to Dr. Knox."

"Oh!" Harry's mouth mirrored the monosyllable.

"But I didn't give them my name. I told them I'd call again from Las Vegas and then meet with a Detective Rogers."

"Did you—?" Keaton began.

"No, no. Not your name or Harry's or what we were driving. I'd never do that. Just a request for an appointment."

"You used your phone, though, right?" Harry asked.

"Yeah…"

"So, they'll have your name from your call, for sure."

"Oh, crap."

"And, of course, your address, social security number, and probably the fact that the Indiana police want you for questioning in Dr. Blackstone's death."

"Holy shit…" Her breath seemed to freeze inside her lungs.

"Which means they may search for your GPS locator, in the phone," Harry's eyes seemed to turn a shade of gray.

"No…"

"Here." He wiggled his fingers toward her. "Give it to me."

Lila reached into her pack and gave Harry her phone. He turned it off then fiddled with the case and pulled the SIM card out, then the battery. "Hand me a sandwich from the cooler, will you?"

"You're hungry now?" She rooted through and pulled one out.

Harry unwrapped the foil from the bread and handed the food back to her.

"What?" she asked.

"See if you can wrap that sandwich with another one in there. Double duty."

She watched him for a moment as he folded the SIM card, battery, and phone separately into the foil, clamping the edges tight.

"That ought to do it." He handed it all back to her. "Let's leave that apart and inside the foil, at least until we get past the New Mexico version of Las Vegas, OK? I mean, just in case."

"It's my turn to feel like shit." She dropped the clump of aluminum into her pack.

"I think none of us should feel like shit," Harry said, looking to Keaton for agreement. "Considering what we've been up against."

"Damn right, Lila."

She sat back and took a disheartened bite from the sandwich, worry spreading like frost across a windowpane.

CHAPTER 41

They drove steadily south, through Springer and Wagon Mound, and when they'd left the city limits of Las Vegas, New Mexico, behind them, Lila felt her stomach unclench a notch. A quick stop for gas and Harry took the wheel for a while. They were soon off the interstate, taking state highways deeper into New Mexico. Route 285 led them across high desert and jagged outcrops and Lila found herself mesmerized by the unusual countryside.

After an hour or so, a sign ahead said: "Roswell – 15 miles."

"Can you see him?" Harry asked.

"Who? A car?" she glanced behind her.

"Yeah. Brown sedan."

Keaton craned his neck, peering through the back window.

Lila raised her right leg onto the seat, twisting back, stretching her arm across the top of the rear bench. "I'm not sure. There might be a brown one behind that semi."

"I'd swear it's been behind us for miles now." Harry looked at her in the rearview mirror. "It might be a Nissan…"

"Not the one that chased us way back in Indiana?" she asked.

Keaton snorted.

She concentrated on the red Peterbilt several car lengths behind them, watching for movement or color behind the large truck. White pipes of some sort were stacked and chained against the truck bed, and it was difficult to see through them. A brown car leaned across the centerline, peeking around the semi, deciding whether to pass, then darted back behind the truck. The road curved gently to their right, making it impossible to see the sedan anymore and unlikely it would try to pass until the road straightened again.

Harry shoved the gas pedal to the floor, rocker arms clattering like a swarm of metal locusts, windows vibrating a snare drum solo, her heart racing with it. Doorhandles and dental fillings rattled inside the old blue tank. They sped faster down the highway, pulling farther and farther away from the giant truck.

"I can't see it now, but earlier it looked like it was going to try to pass the semi," she shouted over the noise of the engine.

Lines in Keaton's forehead deepened.

The road rose before them, slowing the Chevy for

a while, then dropping them quickly toward a giant bowl in the landscape. A sign with a painted green alien face and giant arrow pointed to a batch of dusty buildings on their right.

"Time to duck and hide." Harry braked hard, shoving them forward in their seats, swiveling Lila's legs straight ahead. She placed her palms on the back of the front seat, bracing against the forward motion.

"We should stay on the highway," Keaton protested.

"Too late now." Harry's arms tensed against the steering wheel.

"Harry?" she nearly shouted. She glanced through the rear window.

The Peterbilt rose behind them as it crested the ridge.

Rubber began to squeal across the pavement as Harry continued to brake, swerving them slightly left, then right, then onto a gravel road leading into a parking lot lined with poplar trees. They flew past the first few trees and Harry braked again, turning quickly toward a row of cars parked outside a large, one-story building painted olive-green. They slowed to a safer speed and Harry took them beyond the other cars and behind the building. He stopped at what looked like a roofless shed that housed a large, fan-spinning air conditioner.

When Harry turned off the engine, the fresh silence seemed to scream at them. They sat for several moments, the engine slowly clicking as it cooled.

"If he was following us, he's not behind us anymore." Harry pointed across the parking lot.

Soot-colored clouds had piled high against the northern sky, dark anvils threatening to drop.

"Rain," Keaton said. "It's going to sound like a metal drum roll in here."

"Is it safe to get out?" Lila asked.

"Let's get the car cover on and head inside for a while. Take a break. But keep a look-out for anything unusual," Keaton said, opening his door.

"That was some tough driving there, Harry." Lila patted him on the shoulder. He grinned at her in the rearview mirror.

Keaton and Harry tucked the form-fitting tarp over the Chevy and it seemed to disappear into the dust behind the building. Lila kept her daypack with her, as had become her habit, and they walked to the front entrance. Twenty or so vehicles were parked in rows. She didn't see a brown Nissan or anyone obviously watching them.

A large, green alien with giant eyes and an ironic smile had been painted on the glass doors, greeting them eagerly. Above the alien read: "Area 51 Museum and Gift Emporium." They entered an open room and approached a young woman by a cash register.

Harry meandered toward the countertop. "How much for the museum?"

"Five each for seniors, ten for adults." She fidgeted with a space-saucer earring on her left lobe.

Harry handed her a twenty and received three tickets.

Lila thanked him and her shoulders relaxed. They seemed to have lost the brown sedan at this weird and otherworldly place.

A shop extended to their right, full of caps, T-shirts, toys, models, and yellow roadway signs warning about an "Alien Crossing." Stylized alien masks printed on cardboard and glued to flat handles were two dollars apiece. The museum entrance was on their left, so they made their way in that direction. Spaceships, beams of light, and watchful eyes of extra-terrestrials created an odd and weightless energy, a tingle of static electricity that lifted the mantle of everyday reality. They were stepping into a science fiction movie, and she looked forward to the distraction.

They pushed their way through strips of clear plastic hanging from the ceiling, some kind of faux contamination barrier. A long hallway appeared, walls and ceiling painted black and speckled with small planets and white-colored stars glowing under black lights. The frosty air conditioning here reminded her that outer space would be deadly cold.

A display recessed into the wall appeared at the end of the hall. Inside, a gray child-like body lay on a gurney, two surgeons poised with scalpels above the nearly human form. A layer of slime coated the alien corpse, an arm and three fingers dangling in the air.

A depiction of humans performing an autopsy on E.T.

Harry and Keaton moved ahead of her, leaving her to stare at the large, black eyes and tiny mouth, wondering at the level of detail in the life-sized model. She imagined herself on that table, about to be dissected by human aliens, and the thought gave her a quick chill.

The next room was open and light, displaying a store front and two mannequins in conversation with each other on a city street. One of the models held a silver piece of metal in his hand. She read the large plaque at the front of the diorama.

An unidentified flying object had crashed on a ranch near Roswell in July of 1947. After a severe thunderstorm, "Mack" Brazel found a shallow trench on his land and wreckage with unusual properties. Brazel reported his findings to the sheriff, who reported it to U.S. Army intelligence. The army claimed the debris was from a weather balloon but a brigadier general on the nearby air force base said that was just a "cover story" to conceal the truth from the public. A nurse on the base reported seeing alien bodies and drew pictures of them for a local mortician, after which the nurse was transferred to England and neither seen nor heard from again.

Interesting.

She wandered past the first display to other depictions of men with shovels and pieces of metal, soldiers and army jeeps, and unusual bodies on operating tables.

More plaques added details about the events, witnesses, and efforts by the army to hide evidence from the public.

She glanced around her, suddenly aware that she was alone in the broad hallway. The corridor curved sharply to the left into another wing of the museum. Harry and Keaton must have moved through more quickly – she could not see them up ahead.

Suddenly, the sound of heavy footsteps echoed in the distance behind her.

CHAPTER 42

She moved quickly to a curve in the pathway and turned back to watch. A mother and two children stepped into view, wandering quietly through the museum. The tallest child screeched "Look!" and jumped up and down, pointing at the spaceship crashed behind an army jeep.

Then two big men squeezed past the family, eyes probing the diorama like searchlights in a prison tower – hunting, scanning the display and the walkway ahead of them. One wore a coat with sewn-on patches, the other was larger, his nose crooked.

The men from the café. The ones who'd admired Keaton's 1960 Bel Air. Or so they'd pretended. They must have wanted someplace less crowded than the restaurant to confront her and Harry and Keaton.

They were walking in her direction.

She spun into the next large room, the pathway straight and long. She could run, but they'd hear her.

Where the hell were Harry and Keaton?

To her right stood a mock-up of an alien space-ship, a silver saucer with holes and lights along its beltway. Alien mannequins seemed to be gathering soil and rock samples from Earth. A waist-high barrier ran the length of the life-sized display, maybe twenty-five yards long. Desert sand lined the ground beneath the ship.

Should she?

Footsteps grew steadily louder.

She hopped the barrier and hurried across the sand on her toes, dodging dried grass and rocks until she reached the area behind the spaceship. There, out of sight from visitors, the display was incomplete. The back of the ship was open, as if the last third of it had been sliced away with a laser beam. The inside was gray and dusty, empty except for wiring that led to lights along the outside center of the ship. She couldn't tell how sturdy the structure might be.

The footsteps seemed to stop.

She glanced at the supports beneath the display. They appeared to be made of metal, like the legs of a kitchen table.

She crept up to the edge and placed her hands on the inside, pushing downward to test the strength of the large model.

The footsteps resumed.

She lifted one leg onto the inside of the display, eas-ing her body gently onto the edge.

The spaceship shifted downward a notch, jarring her.

The footsteps gathered speed.

She rolled farther into the display and stopped, searching the museum walkway through the holes in the craft. Though partially blocked by Christmas lights, she could see motion to her left, at the entrance to the exhibit.

She held her breath.

Dark forms moved to her right, then left, then crossed each other as they examined the alien craft.

The spaceship dropped another half inch into the sand, her weight much more than the designer had intended the structure to support.

The two dark forms stopped in their tracks. One of them moved closer to the saucer, his bulk blocking the lamps behind him. She caught a glimpse of his pinched nose, reddened under the spaceship lights, and he leaned closer to the ship, hanging across the barrier, eyes searching the display, head canting this way and that, and just when she was sure he'd discovered her, a child's voice squealed with delight.

"Mommy! An alien spaceship!"

A tired mother shuffled behind the vocal child, an even younger toddler in tow.

"A spaceship, a spaceship!" The child placed an aluminum foil hat onto his head, positioning it to best protect against extraterrestrial technology.

The man shook his head and leaned back toward

the walkway.

She released her breath slowly.

The child pushed his way close to the men and they avoided the boy like he was radioactive, backing away, walking past the display and into the next room.

She rolled gently out of the back, touching her toes to the ground, lifting herself from the display. Maybe she could follow the two men; turn the tables on them. She needed to find Harry and Keaton.

She walked from behind the spacecraft, dusting herself as she went.

"Mommy! A girl from a spaceship!"

The mother's mouth hung open, her disbelief in the alien story momentarily shaken.

Lila waved quickly and nodded in embarrassment. She hopped the barrier and slid her feet across the concrete floor toward the entrance of the next display.

CHAPTER 43

Lila peered around the corner.

A galaxy full of suns and planets hung from a night-black ceiling, neon lights casting an eerie glow across the orbs. A row of busts along the walkway displayed a variety of alien heads, some elongated, others balloon shaped, some eyes round, others like almonds.

The man with the narrow nose moved purposefully along the display, his partner close behind.

Keaton stood at the end of the room, hands behind his back, examining one of the busts. Lila couldn't see Harry.

She had to warn them.

She hurried into the room as the first man drew Keaton's attention. The man pulled his right fist back, a spring-loaded weapon ready to strike.

Keaton's feet shifted into a stance, hips toward the first man, shoulders turned.

"Watch out!" she yelled.

The second man turned toward her and glared.

The first man swung hard at Keaton, who leaned away, dodging the blow. Then Keaton slid his right foot forward and punched the man squarely beneath the ribs, then again, and the man stopped all movement for a second or two and his arms dropped to his side, his knees seemed to melt underneath him, and he collapsed onto the concrete floor in a heap.

The second man turned back toward Keaton, fists tight in anticipation, and slid forward. Keaton retreated a step, keeping the distance between them.

Harry appeared from behind one of the alien busts and pulled it from its pedestal. He ran toward the man, alien skull raised in the air, and brought it down on the man's head with a crash.

The second man dropped to the floor.

Harry reached for another bust and pulled a rubber mask off the skull. He tugged the alien visage over the second man's head.

"Oh my god, are you guys OK?" Lila ran to them, stepping around the two men on the floor.

"Sure." Harry grinned.

Keaton nodded and relaxed out of his stance.

"Army training?" she asked.

"Genwakai," Keaton said.

"Karate," Harry explained.

"A few decades ago, but still…"

"Time to exit." Harry waved for them to follow and hurried toward a black hole painted on the wall, an emergency exit to another multiverse.

The first man seemed to be breathing rapidly as he lay on the floor, knees to his chest. The second man sat upright, feeling his way along the ground, blinded by the rubber mask.

She ran behind Harry and Keaton as they pushed the door open, daylight flooding the corridor.

"Mommy! This is 'da best museum ever!"

She turned to see the older child pointing at the second man, an alien struggling to stabilize himself in Earth's unfamiliar gravity, tugging on his neck as if to remove his head. Despite his desperate efforts, he was not quite getting the hang of it.

CHAPTER 44

She shielded her eyes from the outdoor glare. They found themselves along the front of the building and ran past the entrance. Harry peeled away, trotting among cars in the parking lot, waving his arm at them.

"Brown Nissan," he said, pointing to the vehicle. He disappeared behind another car for a moment, then rose again and hurried to rejoin them.

They ran to the wooden structure that housed the air conditioning and Keaton quickly pulled the tarp from the Bel Air and tossed it in the trunk. Lila jumped into the back seat and slid her daypack onto the floor. Harry took the passenger seat in front. Keaton hopped behind the wheel and started the engine. He slammed his door closed, buckled up, and backed the car from the building. The old car clunked into drive and the rear tires spun gravel into the air.

They rounded the parking lot, tearing past the

parked cars and onto the road that led to the highway. Lila craned her neck to watch behind but could not see anyone coming after them.

Keaton pulled onto the pavement and floored the Chevy, which took nearly two minutes to reach sixty-five miles per hour and, by the time it had, the Area 51 Museum and Gift Emporium was well behind them.

Lila tapped Harry on the shoulder, her question implicit.

"I flattened one of their tires," he grinned. "Ought to take them a good twenty minutes to change it."

"Nice move," she said. "And you guys." She pointed her chin at Harry and then at Keaton. "Who knew you could take out those two goons?"

"Not bad for a couple of old guys, huh?" Harry smiled.

"That's not what I meant."

"But not bad, huh?"

"Hell yeah, not bad! I'm impressed. I mean, I had no idea—"

"He's the tough guy." Harry nodded toward Keaton. "I mean, really. You always want this guy on your side."

"I want both of you on my side."

"Those guys were lying to us when they met us in the café," Harry said.

"Obviously," Keaton agreed.

"Why did they do that? Why did they come up and

talk to us at all?" she asked.

"I think they realized that we'd seen them." Keaton glanced at her. "Then those police officers – highway patrol – walked in behind them. They had to decide right then whether to pretend they weren't really looking at us or run with it and make up a story. The Bel Air gave them an easy excuse why they would be looking for us, an innocent sounding reason."

"So, we'd just forget about them…" she mused.

"Right," Keaton said.

"And find a quieter place to jump us," she added.

"What I can't figure out," Harry said, "is how they found us again."

They rode in silence for several moments.

"Remember how Johnny's guys found us? With those GPS units?" Harry asked.

Keaton nodded.

"Let's pull over next chance we get. I think we should look for a tracking device on the car. Those guys could have put one on really easily when we were eating at the diner."

"Or Neville put one on, in case we got away from him," Keaton said. "If there was a GPS on the car at the diner, I think those guys would have found us at Neville's pretty quickly."

"You're right. If there's a unit on us now, it must be Neville's dirty work."

"Cheeky bastard," Lila imitated Neville's accent.

Keaton turned into the next gas station they saw. He got out of the car and began filling the tank while Harry searched the front and rear bumpers and wheel wells. Lila used the restroom and when she returned, Harry and Keaton were waiting for her. She slid into the back seat again and they rolled slowly out of the gas station and back onto the highway.

"Well?" she asked.

"Found one behind the front tire," Harry said. "Magnetized. So, I put it on one of the fuel pumps. They'll get that far and lose us."

"Nice," she said.

"From now on, I'm checking for those damn things every time we stop," Harry said.

"But they'll know what general direction we're going," Keaton said. "And we're going straight south to Carlsbad then on to El Paso."

"So, we'll have to keep an eye out for them," Harry said.

"That still doesn't answer the key question." She tucked her hair behind her ears. "They're not the goons who work for Johnny, so...who they hell are they and who do they work for and what do they want?"

"They want you, darlin'." Harry gave her a sad smile. "Has to be. They have to want those seeds or maybe who we're trying to find – that Frances Knox lady."

"I still wish we could call law enforcement," Keaton began.

Harry shook his head.

"Not the feds." Keaton raised a finger. "But the lo-cal sheriff."

Harry glared at him. "Are you forgetting some-thing?" He nodded at Lila.

"No, I know." He tapped the steering wheel. "The visa problem. And the pot. We need to get rid of the pot first, for everyone's sake." He pointed at Harry. "ASAP."

"I talked with Johnny earlier, and we got it all worked out. An alternate time and place for delivery."

"Don't talk to me about Johnny…" Keaton clenched his hands on the wheel. "I don't trust that guy for a second."

"He won't hurt us, Keaton," Harry glanced at Lila. "I told him about the guys trying to steal from him. He trusts us. We'll get rid of those bags near El Paso and be done with him forever."

Keaton grunted, a skeptic.

"I've got the directions." Harry lifted a folded pa-per from his pocket then slid it back into place. "An aban-doned ranch called Split Rock, not far from Fabens. I'll call Johnny a couple of hours before we'll get there, and Chris will meet us there."

"Chris?" Keaton asked.

"I don't know him, but that's his name. We deliver the pot, and he pays me the other five hundred Johnny owes me for travel expenses. Johnny leaves the $6,000 at a hidden spot at my house, there for me when I get back.

Then I'm all clear of my debt with Johnny and we never do business again."

"We just have to get there," Lila said, determination in her voice.

"Right," Harry said.

"But I need to try to contact Frances Knox again, you guys. I left a message, back at the hotel, but she hasn't called me back."

"Could be spotty phone service here and there," Harry said.

"Should we unwrap our cell phones, out of the foil? Use them again?" she asked.

"No." Keaton shook his head.

"I'll see if I can get us a burner phone." Harry pointed at a convenience store and Keaton pulled quickly into the parking lot. He left Lila and Keaton sitting there, watching as a camper truck pulled to a pump for gas. A little girl and her grandfather hurried across the lot and into the store. A few minutes later, Harry came out, small bag in hand.

"Here." Harry pulled open the packaging, turned on the phone, and handed it to Lila.

"We throw it away when we're done?" she asked.

"If we reach Knox and talk to her, I suppose that's what we should do," Harry said.

"Shame to waste the money, but..." She held the phone in her hand and dialed, listening to it ring on the other end.

A woman's voice with a slight southern accent answered, "Hello?"

"Oh, hello, this is Lila, Dr. Blackstone's assistant. I left you a message a while back?"

Harry and Keaton moved closer to Lila so they could hear.

"Yes, I have your message, Lila. How can I be of help?"

"I didn't get to tell you everything. Well, I didn't want to just leave a message…"

"Yes?"

"About those seeds, well…" Harry put his hand on her shoulder. "Dr. Blackstone was murdered, you see, shot by someone trying to get them."

"Oh…" Knox's voice trailed into silence, and they waited for her to say something else. "That's, that's terrible…"

"I know and I would tell you in person, but we need to warn you. Whoever shot Dr. Blackstone's been chasing after us and if they know we're coming to deliver the seeds to you, you could be in danger, too."

"Oh…yes. I see."

Lila tried to slow her breathing. "How well did you know Dr. Blackstone?"

"Yes, I've known him for years. We went to school together for a while and we co-authored a paper…I…"

She let Knox's silence drift through the moment.

"We have your post office box," Lila said, "but we

don't have your physical address. Dr. Blackstone wanted me to deliver these seeds to you."

"Do you know why?"

"We think we've figured it out, Dr. Knox."

"Call me Franny."

"Franny. We think Dr. Blackstone developed a chokecherry plant that absorbs almost a thousand times more CO_2 than the American sweetgum tree."

"Yes, yes. He'd said as much to me in his message. Before…"

"Right. We're headed to Fabens now."

"We?"

"I'm with a couple of friends. They have a quick stop at an abandoned ranch just a little north of there."

"Abandoned ranch?"

"Yeah…"

"Let me think about a good place to meet you and I'll call you back, Lila. On this number?"

"No, we've had some…complications with my phone." She grimaced. "I'll call you later. I'm so glad I finally reached you. It's so good to hear your voice. Dr. Blackstone wanted you to have these plants. He must have known that you'd know what to do with them."

"Oh. Yes, indeed. Call me back soon."

"Thank you, Franny."

"No, no. Thank you."

CHAPTER 45

The sandy road meandered toward a blank horizon, the landscape speckled with sage brush and moon rocks, as foreign as any place Lila'd ever been. Dirt roads seemed to appear out of nowhere, cross their path then disappear, "two-tracks" Keaton called them, wandering all over the place. They'd followed detailed directions from Johnny toward a new rendezvous, a new location for delivery of the two large dry bags full of premium marijuana. Someplace Johnny's double-crossing goons would not expect. Despite their reconciliation, it was still a sore spot between Harry and Keaton – they hadn't talked much more about the task at hand. They all just wanted it to be done with.

She'd watched out the rear window of the old Bel Air for signs that anyone had been following them and, except for a spit of dust now and then, no one seemed close to them.

A lip of ground appeared across a shallow valley of sorts and their route turned quickly downward. They passed a jumble of rock on their left then saw a ribbon of green below the rim, grass, and cottonwoods hugging a shallow swath of moisture. Another dirt road snaked into the hollow from the other direction. Farther on, an old homestead rose from the dust, its wooden sides dry and gray as bone. Just beyond the abandoned house rose a large barn, the northern side still shaded with red paint that must once have coated the whole building. The route dropped them to the bottom of the basin. The road wandered, then curved in a half circle to their left, crossing an empty ditch, running toward some sand hills for a few yards. The route turned back, crossing the same ditch farther down. From there, the road straightened toward the house, a make-shift porch sagging from the front like a smock about to drop from an old woman's waist. Windows hung on either side of the door, tired eye sockets, planks drooping alongside its face.

A silver truck rolled slowly from the left side of the house.

Lila's stomach clenched.

The truck stopped fifty feet away, headlights on even under the blazing sun. The lights went out, a signal of peace between them, at least for now. Keaton pulled the Bel Air to face the truck and stopped.

Harry nodded at her and Keaton, lips tight, eyes narrowed, and then his face pulled into a friendly façade.

He suggested they sit still and keep their hands in the air. He slid from the front seat, arms raised, and yelled a hearty "hello."

Two men slid from the truck and pushed cowboy hats onto their heads. One walked slowly toward Harry, who had stopped in front of the Chevy. The other man moved to the side of his pickup. A third man stayed in the driver's seat. A fourth man stood in the bed of the truck, shotgun resting on top of the cab.

A whole army of drug-dealing cowboys. Where were the Indians when you needed them?

The first man strode toward Harry and nodded. "Where?"

Harry waved for him to follow, and they walked to the trunk of the Chevy. Harry fumbled with the key and opened the trunk. Lila felt weight shifting as the large dry bags were removed. The trunk lid remained raised, but she could hear locks being removed, contents pulled and shifted, bags re-sealed.

"We appreciate your honesty in this transaction," the man said.

"Keep a close eye. Those double-crossing goons of Johnny's have managed to find us at least once on our trip down here."

"Don't worry about us."

Harry closed the trunk.

The man nodded toward his pickup and the man waiting there by the front grille trotted to the back of the Chevy.

The first man pulled an envelope from his pocket and handed it to Harry. She figured that must be the $500 travelling money. He lifted his hand in the air, a signal to the driver, who pulled what looked like a satellite phone to his ear.

The driver spoke for a moment and nodded to the first man.

"Funds transferred to Johnny," the first man told Harry.

Each of the two men lifted one of the dry bags onto their backs, arms tucked beneath the shoulder straps. They crossed the ground in front of the Bel Air, moving toward their pickup.

Harry shuffled to the door of the Chevy.

Lila released a long sigh then pulled fresh air into her lungs, feeling her shoulders relax.

Gunfire exploded from the far side of the old house, shotgun blasts and pistols, air concussing in chaos.

CHAPTER 46

Harry reached into her door, yanking her pack, which she wore on her arm, pulling her across the back seat and out into the open air.

What was he doing?

"Up, up, go!" he shouted, pointing behind the Bel Air.

Keaton was already out, running toward the trunk.

She froze for a moment, hands on her ears. The man in the bed of the silver pickup spun toward the house, firing once, then fell out of sight. The two men who'd gathered the pot ran to the far side of the pickup, tossing the drybags into the rear cab, scrambling inside. Their hats lay on the ground.

The driver seemed to be slumping forward, but the truck slid into gear and began to turn away from the shooters. The driver must be ducking out of sight.

Harry pushed her toward the rear bumper.

Keaton yelled: "There!"

They led her away from the Chevy toward an old well that stood between the house and the barn, a bare circle of rocks on the open ground.

They spun behind the wall of stones and peered back.

The pickup tore across the dusty ground, bouncing over knobs and ruts, retreating toward the road that had led them into the shallow drainage.

Two men strode from behind the far wall of the house, backs toward Lila and Keaton and Harry. They fired toward the silver truck, triggers pulled in the heat of the action, celebrating their victory.

They must be Johnny's goons, one with a shotgun, one with two pistols in his hands, old west style.

They seemed high on something, crazed with a kind of fever.

Harry looked behind them, toward the barn. He took a step away, ready to run, but Keaton grabbed his shirt.

"Look," he whispered.

The men had turned, examining the Chevy from several yards away, shuffling toward it cautiously. Harry ducked back down behind the well.

If they ran now, the men would see them.

Lila lowered herself to the ground and peeked from the edge of the rock wall.

One man was large and round, the one Harry had

called Meatball. The other was shorter but well-muscled, too, with a shotgun in the crook of his arm. Cole. The men quickly seemed to realize the Chevy was empty of people and moved to the trunk. Cole set his shotgun against the bumper and lifted the lid, searching frantically, tossing gear and boxes onto the ground. Meatball raised a pistol into the air and fired at the sun.

The shot was an electric needle, jabbed into her skin.

"Damn it, damn it, we're too late!" Cole yelled to his partner. "They've taken the pot!"

"Shit, man, we've got to go after them."

"We'll never catch them now." Cole waved an arm at the truck barreling out of the arroyo.

The men just stood there, shock on their faces, short fuses sizzling fast.

"We'll still find them quick enough." Meatball lowered his pistol and turned toward the well and beyond.

"Still, it's a pain in the ass," Cole muttered.

Meatball scanned the ground, searching. "We still have three witnesses to take care of…"

"Did they make it to the barn?" Cole picked up his shotgun.

"Let's find out."

They moved about twenty feet from each other and began walking toward the well, eyes focused on the rough rock wall. Lila slipped back behind the edge.

Harry rose slowly beside her, arms in the air. "I'm here," he said, his words wholly unnecessary. "My friends made it past the barn." He pointed away.

"Oh, I doubt that, buddy." Meatball's boots clomped across the dirt.

What was Harry thinking?

Cole's feet shuffled sideways around the well until the inevitable arrived.

Lila put her daypack on the ground and she and Keaton rose, hands in the air.

"We've even got the perfect burial site," Meatball spoke to his partner.

"What?" Cole asked, bulging eyes darting from side to side, ever ready, it seemed, to lose their synchronization.

Meatball waved one of his guns at the center of the empty well.

CHAPTER 47

"I got an idea," Cole said. "Let's all sit on the side of the well," he told Lila, Keaton, and Harry, aiming his shotgun at Keaton's gut.

"What?" Meatball asked.

"We shoot 'em into the well, we don't have to lift them up and in."

"Brilliant," Meatball said, a lop-sided grin on his lips.

Cole motioned with his gun.

Keaton lowered his arms to the wall of the well and sat on its edge.

"Turn round," Cole ordered. "Feet in the well."

Keaton did as he was told.

Harry and Lila sat on the outside of the well.

"Hey, guys, you know me," Harry began. "We've both worked for Johnny, you know, for years now. There's no need for this…"

Cole stepped closer and aimed the shotgun at Harry.

"Hey, man, at least tell me one thing before you shoot me, Cole. How did you guys keep finding us?"

"GPS."

"No, I took them out of the bags," Harry shook his head. "Dropped 'em in a sheriff's truck so you'd follow it instead of us."

"That did throw us off track for a while. 'Till we figured it out. But those units were on top of the pot." Meatball sneered.

"We put an old GPS in the bottom of one of the bags, too," Cole said. "Just in case. Wrapped in a towel."

Harry remembered that Johnny had "lost" a GPS on his workbench, before they'd begun their trip. "Not under the bumper?" He asked.

Cole shook his head.

"Brilliant, man, really smart." Harry tried to smile. "We could do a helluva business if we team up…"

"Shut up," Meatball said.

"Come on, now, Meatball," Harry intoned, "Cole. We know each other. We work hand in glove with Johnny…"

Cole strode within inches of Harry's face, shotgun aimed at his throat. "We could always gut shoot you and leave you to the blackbirds and the coyotes." Cole moved closer to Lila. "And do the same with this cute thing, Harry, and your pal Keaton here. Do as we say, and it will be over quick, before you even feel the pain."

Lila's mind seemed to be soaking in cement, dropping into heavy denial, some kind of shock.

Harry's lips pressed together, eyes tight as slits. "Let her alone, guys, she's just a hitchhiker who needed a ride. She has nothing to do with Johnny or your business. Or ours…"

Keaton slid slowly to the outer edge of the rock wall.

"Turn around on the side and put your feet into the well," Cole ordered.

Harry nodded and began to lift his legs. In quiet disobedience, Keaton scooted farther toward the outside edge.

Shit. Harry and Keaton were going to make a move – they were going to run at these guys and get blown away in the process.

"Wait." Lila lifted her hands farther in the air. "What if I told you I have some of the finest seeds ever harvested? Genetically engineered seeds…"

Meatball squinted toward her, a skeptic with a scintilla of doubt that she might not be lying. "Yeah?" he asked.

"Yeah." She nodded, speaking the literal truth. "Genetically engineered for potency you'll never find anywhere else. The start of the most profitable enterprise you'll ever imagine."

"Where?"

"I'll tell you where, but you have to promise to let us go."

"Oh, come on…"

"No, really, think about it, Meatball," Harry said. "We can't rat on you guys even if we wanted to – we'll all spend twenty years in jail for that delivery, you know that!"

Meatball hesitated.

"We can't waste any more time with this shit," Cole said. "We've gotta grab that pot back from those guys in the truck or we're dead in the water."

"You'll just follow the GPS that's still in the bag…" Keaton said.

"Right, genius," Cole replied.

Meatball seemed to shake himself out of a stupor. "Right. We'll find those seeds after you're all in the bottom of the well."

Cole stepped closer to them. "Move to the edge of the well. Now."

Keaton's courage seemed to collapse. He slid back into position and hung his feet over the inside of the well.

Harry slowly followed.

Lila stared into Cole's shotgun, the lifeless, double-barreled eyes of the devil himself aimed at her soul. She slid onto the rock wall and swung her feet over the edge, moving as if she were but a marionette.

In a final fit of defiance, she decided she'd jump into that well before she'd let them shoot her dead and, as that thought surged through her, she looked at Harry and Keaton and their sad eyes met. Had they decided the same thing, too?

Did she have time for one last breath?

Cole walked behind Keaton and lifted the shotgun to his shoulder.

CHAPTER 48

An eruption like the blast of a jet engine struck the air but instead of Keaton falling into the well, he slipped backward, clumsily, onto the ground. Lila and Harry crashed with him, hardened dirt striking her shoulder, a rapid percussion of fire blasting into a single, deafening roar.

And then it stopped, her ears ringing.

Keaton scrambled across the dust, pulling Harry with him, to a position near Lila behind the well, away from the source of the blast.

Cole's body was wrenched in two, a pulpy, bloody mass with an upper half and a lower half separated unnaturally, viscera and blood smeared across the middle, dollops of liver and lung quivering in the sand, human gristle steaming in the air.

She turned away, swallowing the urge to vomit.

She peered along the other side of the well and there lay Meatball, pistols still in his hands, eyes pulled tight, groaning, blood flowing from his stomach as the life within him spilled into the sand.

Her joints seemed to melt, her ligaments unstrung. Hell.

What had happened?

Had someone just saved them from Johnny's goons?

She took a gulp of air.

Keaton handed her the daypack and motioned with his fingers for them to run and in that moment all rational thought abandoned her, but her muscles quickly found their purpose, her strength returned.

They ran in a crouch, the stone wall between them and the shooters. Keaton led the way, then Lila, Harry trailing behind, and when they'd covered nearly twenty feet, single shots rang out behind them, puffs of dust blown into the air to her left and they ran faster and faster until suddenly they dropped into the ditch that ran in front of the old homestead, the one they'd crossed twice along the road.

They crashed into each other at the bottom, frantic to keep moving. Keaton raised his hands, signaling for calm. He helped her slide her arms through the straps and shoulder her pack.

"We can run along the ditch!" Keaton said.

The shooting had stopped. The silence fed her fears more than the cacophony that had come before, her breath coming in short, sharp gasps.

Harry held her face in her hands, willing her to

watch his eyes, willing her to slow her heartbeat. She nodded her thanks and took a deeper breath.

"Let's go!" Keaton waved them forward.

Her feet pounded the ground as if her shoes weighed twenty pounds apiece, jarring her forward. Keaton kept the lead and Harry followed behind her. They weaved past branches and stones in the dry irrigation ditch as the trench curved left, toward the faded barn they'd seen when they'd arrived.

Someone shouted behind them, the words unclear, sounds echoing up the ditch.

Keaton reached a spot where cows or deer had forged a short trail out of the ditch and toward the barn, now looming ahead of them. He hurried up the incline and knelt at the top. She stopped at the bottom of the path, hands on her knees, panting hard.

Keaton motioned them up and ran toward the barn.

She and Harry followed, sprinting through the grass to a door on the side of the building. Keaton crashed into the wooden frame, fumbled with the latch, then slid inside and held the door open. She and Harry rushed inside and Harry closed the door behind them.

Sunlight filtered between slats in the walls, a fine dust visible in vertical strips across the open space. Empty stalls aligned to their right; wooden pens four feet high with sturdy gates gnawed across the tops by the teeth of nervous horses long gone.

"Can we hide?" she asked.

"See if there's a way out of the back." Harry pointed behind her.

She trotted across the barn, past a decrepit, ox-driven wagon. Keaton and Harry fanned out along the other walls, all of them searching, listening. Bales of dry hay were stacked along the far side, some of them pulled part way across the ground, as if to be loaded and taken away. She made her way around them toward the rear of the barn but stopped at a series of planks spread across the ground. She lifted one of the pine boards and it pulled away from a frame with hinges on the side. A doorway. To more storage? To a root cellar, maybe?

She sat on the ground at the edge and stared into the dark hole. If she was right, the cellar was about six feet deep.

She glanced about and listened for Harry or Keaton but could not see or hear them. She turned to face the edge, placed her hands there, and lowered her legs into the hole, and just when she thought she'd misjudged the distance, her toes felt something solid. Her chest scraped down the earthen wall and she came to rest on the bottom. She could see the top of a nearby bale of hay and the inside roof of the barn, but the rest was beyond her view.

Her eyes adjusted to a faint light radiating into the room but deeper in, the hole was black as oil. She felt her way along the wall, careful to lift her feet high and set them down slowly. Her toes bumped against loose boards, but the cellar appeared otherwise empty. She found the back wall, rough and solid.

The cellar had no exit outside of the barn.

She made her way back to the spot where she'd lowered herself into the hole. She needed to climb out and find the guys.

The voice of an unfamiliar man echoed through the chamber, stern and curt: "Tie them to the post."

CHAPTER 49

Someone brushed against a bale of hay.

Lila stepped backward into the dark.

"Hey, is that you, Lila?"

It was a woman's voice, tinged with a slight southern accent.

"We know you're here…" the woman's legs appeared above the root cellar and stopped. "Hey, are you down there?"

Was it Franny Knox? Had she killed Johnny's goons?

"Hey, I can help you and your friends, but we need to talk again…"

She had no more doubt that it was Knox.

"After you called, I checked on the internet and sure enough, there was a story about him, that he'd been killed…"

Should Lila answer?

"I was so sorry to hear about Blackstone. We'd been

colleagues, years ago, you know. But we're in a tough spot here. A little cooperation from you would really help."

Lila stepped into the weak light. "I'm here."

Knox knelt toward the cellar. "Oh, thank god."

"How did you find me?"

"Your message said you'd be at an abandoned ranch north of my place. Split Rock is a well-known rancheria in the area, so we took a chance."

We?

Knox shifted into a more comfortable squat. "I need to test those seeds, Lila, to see what Dr. Blackstone discovered."

Lila could see part of the woman's body, but not her face.

"Where are Keaton and Harry?"

"Up here. They're fine."

"Who shot those men, out by the old well?"

"Awful, wasn't it? They're with me. There are at least three ways in and out of this empty rancheria. It's known to be used for drug deals. I brought help with me in case we ran into trouble. We saved your lives."

True enough. But she'd also heard a man tell some-one to tie up Harry and Keaton. "Send Harry over to talk to me."

Knox waited a beat, motionless, then released a long sigh. "Listen, Lila, that's not going to happen. I need those seeds. Dr. Blackstone wanted me to have them. He told me what he'd discovered."

"When did he call you?"

"He left me a message the night before he died. He was sending the seeds to me. I told Keith Wormwood, who runs Dragontree Agri-Economics, a genetic engineering management company. I do some consulting for him. He's the one who will protect and develop this discovery, Lila."

"His men killed those guys, out by the well?"

"They had to. To save you and your friends."

"His men killed Dr. Blackstone?"

Knox took a deep breath, avoiding the question. "Dr. Blackstone needs me to test the seeds and the plants, once they've grown. I need to verify his findings. And if he's right, those seeds could help reverse the climate disaster we're facing. It's critical for all of us."

Lila gritted her teeth and retreated farther into the cellar. "I don't trust you."

"Dr. Blackstone trusted me. Please, you've got them with you, don't you?" She extended her hand toward the edge of the underground room. "Give me those seeds."

Knox was no longer asking – she was directing.

Lila knelt to the floor and felt in the dirt until she found one of the loose boards she'd stepped on earlier.

"Listen," Knox said, voice softening again. "We had to team up with some folks to help us, and they are not the forgiving type, if you know what I mean. If you don't hand me those seeds, they will hurt your friends."

"They'll do what you tell them."

"Mr. Wormwood is the boss, Lila, and he's not budging on this."

Lila released her fingers from the board.

"You saw what they did to those drug dealers. They will break bones, noses, eye sockets, if they have to. Please don't mess with them."

Lila raised herself from the cellar floor.

"I can't guarantee what they'll do to your friends if we don't get those seeds." Knox reached her hand into the cellar and wiggled her fingers, urging Lila to deliver.

The earthen room seemed to close around her, a deep and dampened grave.

"Give me those seeds. Now." Knox leaned closer to the cellar and peered inside, her faded eyes glazed as marbles.

Lila's throat swelled and seized in place.

"The seeds for the lives of your friends." Her lips barely moved, her face as still as a liar's mask.

What choice did Lila have?

Her feet seemed to sink into the floor, numbness spreading from her toes to her ankles to her calves, and her mouth was so dry she could not even release a squeak.

CHAPTER 50

A man's footsteps crossed the ground and stopped behind Knox. "What's going on?" he asked.

"Get Mr. Wormwood over here, would you?" Knox leaned away from the cellar entrance and stood, her feet next to the bale of hay.

The man turned and walked away. A few moments later, another set of footsteps shuffled close to Knox.

"She's not coming out and she's not giving me the seeds," Knox said.

"No problem," Wormwood said. "Byron!"

Lila heard the shuffle of feet.

"Do your thing." Wormwood walked away from Knox.

The sound of a man grunting in pain reached the cellar and she knew it was Keaton. These men were beating him.

"Stop!" Lila yelled to Knox. "Stop now. I'll give

you the seeds."

"Mr. Wormwood!" Knox yelled.

More feet shuffled across the ground, but she heard no more sounds from Keaton or Harry.

Lila slid the pack from her shoulders and rested it on the ground. She pulled the zipper apart and reached inside.

Knox squatted low to the entrance and reached her hand forward again. "All we need are the seeds and we can all go home." Her voice had a chill to it.

Lila lifted the bag of chokecherries, feeling the weight of it.

She released a painful whine, a breath of despair.

She and Keaton and Harry had lost.

Knox's fingers lowered into the cellar again, beckoning impatiently.

Lila handed the baggie to Knox and there, alone in the damp and dark, tears rolled across her cheeks and down her neck, the earth swallowing her whole.

After all this time…she and Keaton and Harry… all they'd done to evade Johnny's goons and the other men she now knew were with Franny Knox and this Mr. Wormwood, people who would kill to get those seeds.

They must truly be worth millions and millions of dollars. At least, to the people or the companies that controlled them. Once the world knew the seeds existed, governments and corporations around the world would pay mightily to get even just a few of them. The initial burst of sales would be astronomical.

Worth killing for. Worth killing Dr. Blackstone. Worth beating her friends.

Her chest ached, each breath shallow and strained.

Knox stood with the bag, only her legs still in view. "Stay put for five minutes, then get yourself and your friends and go home." She shuffled out of view.

Lila moved to the edge of the cellar for a better view, ready to yell to Keaton and Harry, when she heard a brushing sound.

Someone was pushing the bale of hay closer to her exit, impeding her escape. She ducked against the wall and waited.

"Let's go," Knox yelled. Feet scurried across the ground, Knox and Wormwood and the others, the barn door banging shut.

A smell like sulfur and tobacco reached Lila's nose and then she saw what it really was.

The bale of hay was on fire.

CHAPTER 51

Footfalls clumped across the ground, away from Lila, and the barn door banged shut again.

"Keaton! Harry!" she yelled.

Muffled voices cried in the distance.

Fire began to climb the side of the bale.

She moved quickly back into the cellar, searching the ground for the boards she'd stepped on before. She found one and brought it back toward the light, pushing it against the block of hay, but it seemed rooted to the floor of the barn.

Flames flashed upward then disappeared as loose strands of chaff burned off the packed bale.

She put one end of the board on her shoulder, aiming it upward, pressing it against the smoldering bundle, shoving with the strength of her legs.

Nothing.

Smoke surged from the opposite side of the hay.

She adjusted her angle and tried again and this time the bale moved two inches away from the cellar exit.

She tried again, sliding it against the ground another two inches, then another two, until her shoulder ached, then past the pain another few inches and she had just enough room to squeeze out of the underground room. She started up then remembered her pack. She slipped it onto her shoulders and put her hands on the edge of the floor above her and jumped. Her arms straightened and she skidded one knee onto the ground level, turning her face from the flames. She stood and teetered on the edge of the cellar a moment then leapt past one corner of the flaming bale, scorching her pants, running toward the center of the barn and beyond, toward the horse stalls.

Keaton and Harry sat side by side, hands behind their backs, rags stuffed into their mouths.

Smoke billowed into the rafters above her.

She slid her pack to the floor and reached inside for a small pair of greenhouse shears she kept there. She reached behind Keaton, snipping the twine that held his hands. Once Keaton was free, she moved to Harry and cut him loose, too. The men pulled the cloths from their mouths.

Fire spread across the floor in a sudden rush, combustion sweeping through loose grass and hay, rising into the wooden frame of the old wagon, sucking oxygen from the air.

Harry coughed and motioned them toward the

barn door.

She reshouldered her pack and covered her mouth with her hand. Smoke crept lower, down and across the ceiling, pushing toward them as they ran for the door.

Harry turned the handle and pushed, rocking the door back and forth, but it would not open. She and Keaton shoved the door in sync with Harry, but it held against their weight.

Wormwood and Knox had blocked the door.

Heat radiated from the burning wagon, smoke lowering toward the tops of their heads.

They stood back from the door then smashed against it again, shaking the frame.

Flames surged through debris along the floor, coming right at them. She tried to stamp it out, choking on the over-heated air.

Harry and Keaton tried again, but the door held strong.

She joined them in another run at the exit, plowing their shoulders into the wood, desperate to escape before the flames burned their shoes, their pants, their very skin.

The door broke open a few inches, daylight just beyond their reach.

Soot began to coat their heads and shoulders, flaking from the burning rooftop. Fumes filled her lungs with molten heat, choking off her breath.

They pushed again, driving their tired shoulders into their prison door, boards bending, nails screeching, timber groaning all around them until slivers of light flashed across her vision and she sunk to her knees and passed out.

CHAPTER 52

Her chest heaved with each cough, no way to control it, until she finally seemed to gather some oxygen and her convulsions slowed. Harry and Keaton were nearby, hacking up phlegm, sucking fresh air into their lungs.

They'd pulled her clear of the burning barn and into the ditch.

She rose to the edge of the dry canal and peered over.

The grizzled building raged like a furnace, flames consuming the desert-dry wood, the roof, the sides, every single piece of every single thing inside.

Her cough subsided slowly, awkwardly. She leaned against the earthen wall and stared at the immense flames, awed, exhausted, relieved. Her face reddened with the heat, so she turned away and squatted below the edge of the ditch where the air was clear and cool.

Harry and Keaton shuffled toward her and gave her a nod of recognition.

"That bastard nailed the door shut," Keaton forced the words before another fit of coughing.

"Franny Knox called him Wormwood," Lila said.

"Right. He had two other guys with him, too." Harry looked to each of them. "They tried to kill us."

His words soaked into her brain and she heaved toward the ground, nothing in her stomach to vomit. Unimaginable. Horrible. Evil. Unfathomable. The words spilled from her mind, and she soon heard herself saying them out loud, spitting them into the air, anger flushing her cheeks.

"Knox and Wormwood were working together all along." Harry knelt below the edge of the ditch.

"But we were bringing the seeds to Knox…" Lila shook her head. "All she had to do was wait for us."

"But she knew others were after us, too," Harry added.

"Johnny's goons…"

"Right."

They could hear the roof rasping and crashing behind them.

Keaton squatted closer to her. "But Knox didn't know they were after Johnny's marijuana. Remember? You told Knox about Johnny's guys. Not by name, or why they were after us, but that we were being followed. Chased. Knox must have figured it was a race for the seeds. She wasn't going to let anyone else get them."

Liars, all of them. Cheats. Greedy, evil, self-important, wicked, immoral bastards. And Knox, the bitch of bitches. Dr. Blackstone had trusted her. They'd all trusted her. Damn it.

Harry sat on his haunches. "And she must have teamed up with Wormwood, who had the muscle and, literally, the fire power, to deal with Johnny's men. And with us, too."

"Oh, god," she looked into Harry's sea-blue eyes. "Oh, hell." She stared at the grass at the bottom of the ditch. Anger melted into despair, fury into anguish. "I gave the seeds to Knox."

CHAPTER 53

Keaton shook his head. "No, Lila, you didn't."

"Yes, guys, I did. I handed the bag of seeds to Knox. She said she'd release all of us, that all she wanted were those seeds and she'd let us go."

Harry's brow rose.

"I knew I couldn't trust her, but I heard someone hurting one of you…"

"Wormwood kicked me in the stomach," Keaton said. "Took me by surprise and kicked the air out of me, but I'm OK."

"I couldn't let them hurt you."

"It's OK," Harry put his hand on her shoulder. "You were fabulous in there! You saved our wrinkly old asses, you did! Cut us free, got us out of there."

"Lila, Harry." Keaton looked to each of them, a subtle smile on his face. "I said 'you didn't give the seeds to Knox'."

"What?" she asked.

"You gave her some chokecherry seeds, that's true." Keaton nodded. "But you gave her my chokecherry seeds, not Blackstone's chokecherry seeds."

"What the hell?" Harry blurted.

"We knew what Johnny's men would do, even though Johnny himself was on our side. But Knox, well, she was a complete unknown. Somebody other than Johnny's guys were after us. It had to be someone who wanted the chokecherry seeds, not the bags of marijuana."

"So, you, what…?" she leaned forward.

"I found chokecherries outside that motel, the Tumble Inn, remember? Got a shirt full and put them in my socks, inside my baggage. Filled up four of them, tied them at the tops. I swapped my seeds for Blackstone's."

"You sneaky bastard," Harry grinned and slapped Keaton on the back. "How I love you, brother!"

"Victory is often achieved by misdirection."

"Holy…" Lila lurched forward, putting Keaton into a full-on, cheek to cheek embrace he couldn't avoid.

Harry hugged the both of them, bouncing on his feet. "You brilliant, sneaky, son of a bitch!"

CHAPTER 54

Timbers smashed to the ground, hot air blowing over them, sparks flying above their heads.

"Let's get to the car." Lila loosened her embrace and they hurried down the ditch, bent at the waist.

They made their way past the stone-sided well, avoiding what remained of Meatball and Cole, then stepped out of the dry furrow, walking steadily toward the blue Bel Air. Behind them, two walls of the barn had collapsed to the ground, flames a steady burn, smoke churning in its own wake.

Keaton opened the trunk of the car and leaned in, pointing to a panel near the rear seat. "There," he nodded. "Tucked behind that strip of metal."

Lila could see one corner of the bag of seeds peeking below its hiding place. "Leave it there." She smiled.

She closed the trunk and walked to the side of the car, glancing at the burning barn, when she noticed a hole in the body of the Bel Air, above and a few inches away from the front door.

"Hey!"

Harry touched the side near the hole then raised the hood to see where the bullet may have lodged. Keaton hurried to see what they were looking at.

Metal curved inward around a small crater and Lila could not resist putting her finger inside to feel it.

"Looks OK," Harry said to Keaton. "Hit the frame in here but didn't get into the engine compartment."

"Lucky," Keaton said.

They examined the rest of the car for more bullet holes, and GPS units, but didn't find any.

Keaton closed the hood. "Let's get out of here."

Once in the car, they backed up a few yards and turned onto the road they'd used to reach the old ranch. Another track ran toward cottonwood trees to the left of the house, probably where Johnny's men had hidden. Knox had said there was more than one way into the place, but the road along the house looked rougher than the one they were on. They crossed the empty ditch once, followed the road's half-circle, and crossed it again. After that, they were soon climbing out of the hollow and up to the surrounding plateau.

Lila rolled down her window, dry breezes wafting through the car. She watched the old homestead drop out of view, the smoke thinning, becoming a lighter shade of ash.

They eventually reached the two-lane highway, where they turned west, toward El Paso. They crested a small rise when a fire truck appeared a mile away, blaring its siren. Keaton pulled onto the shoulder until the firemen passed, its alarm trailing into the distance.

"Glad we got off the dirt road before they came along," Lila said. "Where are we heading?"

"Let's hit I-25 in El Paso and see how far north we can get." Keaton leaned forward, intent on the road ahead.

"What about the Chevy place? The restoration shop?" Harry asked. "Aren't they south or east of here?"

"Yeah, you've got a deal to sell the car," Lila said.

Keaton was quiet for a moment.

Harry and Lila glanced at each other.

"I want some time to think about it." Keaton looked at each of them. "Right now, today, I don't want to turn around and go back toward Fabens, toward Knox and those people..."

"I'm glad you said that," Harry agreed. "It gives me creeps to even think about driving back in that direction."

"What are we going to do, then?" Lila tucked loose hair behind her ears.

Harry slid a knee onto the seat, facing her. "Johnny's goons are dead." His words lay a hush on them. "And, the good thing is, Knox and Wormwood must think we're dead, too."

"Those bastards tried to kill us," Lila said.

"First," Keaton began, "we've got to contact the FBI and tell them what happened down at the ranch."

"Hell, brother, that's the last thing we need to do," Harry insisted. "Literally, the last thing…"

Lila leaned forward. "What are you thinking about, Harry?"

CHAPTER 55

"Hand me some water, will you, Lila? From the cooler back there…"

She gave him a bottle and a pack of peanut butter crackers and got some for herself.

"Let's get back to the good news. First, we're all OK with Johnny," Harry began.

"Thank god," sarcasm seeped through Keaton's voice.

Harry ignored him. "Second, Knox and Wormwood think we're dead and – thanks to Keaton and The Art of War – they think they have Blackstone's seeds, too."

Lila nodded.

"Third, we have the actual seeds. Not Knox, not Wormwood, not anybody else."

"We delivered your pot to Johnny's customer." Lila raised a finger.

"Yes," Harry spoke through the dry crackers in his

mouth. "We're good with Johnny and with his buyer."

"We're no longer transporting $120,000 worth of illegal marijuana," Keaton's voice was stiff.

"I've apologized for that, Keaton…"

"Hey," Lila interjected, "we don't really know who Wormwood is. What are his plans for the seeds?"

"Corporate guy, no doubt," Harry said. "He probably planned to corner the market. I mean, once it gets out what Blackstone did, corporations and governments will be tripping over themselves to get those seeds."

"But Wormwood will try to sell the wrong seeds," she said. "Might create some problems for him."

"Poor guy." It was Harry's turn for sarcasm.

"They're worth millions," Keaton agreed.

"What if they claim those seeds will completely reverse global climate change?" Lila asked.

"You said that's not true, didn't you?" Harry said. "Didn't you say those plants could help stem the tide, but they wouldn't let us keep on pouring CO_2 into the air. We'd still have to transition to solar, wind, maybe even back to nuclear power, right?"

"Right."

"So, whatever we do, we have to make sure we get the message out. We can't let the vested interests and their politicians turn this gift from Dr. Blackstone into an excuse to keep polluting the planet." Harry swallowed a gulp of water.

"Do we hand the seeds over to the government? To

that Department of Agriculture guy who funded part of Dr. Blackstone's research?" she asked.

"Trust the government?" Harry's right brow rose above the other.

"Wait... I know what we have to do." She twisted the lid off her bottle of water. "How do plants survive and spread? The seeds are dispersed – by birds and mammals and other means. You and Johnny know all kinds of pot growers, don't you? People with small fields or basement nurseries, gardeners who know how much light to use, the right kind of soil, the right amount of water..."

"Sure." Harry put another cracker into his mouth.

"Then we trust ourselves. And your pals."

"What do you mean?" Harry mumbled.

"We take these seeds to the small-time pot growers and their trusted friends, and we leave a few seeds with them here and there, and we drive north along the Rocky Mountains, where chokecherries really thrive, and we plant, and we disperse the seeds all along the mountains."

Harry's eyes grew round. "Like Johnny Appleseed."

"Right. We disperse the seeds, all but a few for ourselves, all up and down the Rockies. No one gets a monopoly. Wormwood's plan to get rich disappears because they'll be available all over the west, then all over the world, for free. A year or two from now, hundreds of plants will become thousands, thousands will become millions. A real 'grassroots' effort by everyone."

"Disperse the seeds, disperse the economic effect."

Harry smiled.

"And disperse the responsibility, so it's not all on our shoulders – it will disperse the risk to us, too," she said.

"Then we tell the government," Keaton said. "After the seeds are out there, after our part is done."

"When no one can stop us." Harry laughed.

"When we've already delivered the antidote." Lila grinned.

CHAPTER 56

They drove through El Paso's tangle of routes and curves and exit-only lanes and past Las Cruzes, 45 miles north. When the traffic began to thin, Lila leaned her head against the top of the front seat and closed her eyes.

"Time to find a hotel for the night," Harry whispered to Keaton.

The next exit advertised fuel and tacos and a chain hotel, so Keaton slid to the off-ramp and turned down the service road. Harry got them a small suite with a roll-away bed, and they trudged into the poorly lit room and tossed their bags on the floor. Harry called the first shower but before her turn arrived, Lila was sound asleep atop the blankets.

****

Morning came like an unwelcome guest, sluggish

and rude, but a hot shower and a clean set of clothes transformed the early caller into an affable mate. Lila needed to buy more clothes soon or get her dirty ones washed and dried. Her hair had been more tangled than usual, and it took a while for her to feel presentable. She gathered her things and stuffed them into the thrift store bag and her daypack. After yesterday's events, even the mundane was engendering joy, each little lift fifty pounds lighter than the day before.

"Coffee house across the parking lot," Keaton waved his thumb in that direction.

Harry held the door open for them.

They found a table and ordered eggs, pancakes, sausages, coffee and, when the food arrived, they ate like linebackers after a football game.

Harry accepted the tab, and they all ordered more coffee.

"Hey, guys." Keaton cleared his throat. "I've been thinking about something and made a decision last night."

Harry looked up at him, waiting.

"I've decided not to sell the Bel Air after all."

"Oh?" Lila asked.

"I'd rather not go back south again, either." Harry wrapped his hands around his mug.

"It's not just that…though that's a helluva good reason all by itself." Keaton hesitated. "It's kind of silly, really…"

"My god, Keaton, you've never been silly in

your life."

"Well, you know, I worked on that car when I was first learning to drive, so it's got some good memories with it and after all we've been doing, I've kind of gotten attached to the thing all over again."

"That's not silly," Lily said.

"It's a very rare car," Harry agreed, "and now it's got a super cool bullet hole in the front. You can't abandon her now."

"I second that motion," Lila said.

"And toast the decision." Harry raised his coffee and they all touched mugs.

Keaton nodded. "I'll call the restoration shop today and tell them I've changed my mind."

"Congratulations," she added.

"We're going to need the Chevy for this new plan, anyway," Harry said. "Speaking of which, I've got a list of who to call this morning." He tapped his forehead.

"People to see along the way?" Lila asked.

"People who love this planet and know how to garden – if you know what I mean. And people who know people we can trust to follow through, nurture the plants, keep their secret, then give the next batch of seeds to their friends."

"I should never have trusted Knox." Lila shook her head.

"None of us suspected she was a rotten apple," Keaton said.

"Blackstone trusted her. So, I did, too." Lila stared at her hands.

"Blackstone made a mistake and we piggy-backed on that," Harry said.

Keaton faced her. "So, after they knew about Johnny's men, Knox and Wormwood decided to move up the timetable on delivery of Blackstone's seeds. Meatball and Cole had another GPS tracker in one of the bags. When they ran into Johnny's goons, well..." his voice trailed off. "They had to try to kill us, too, at that point. We were witnesses."

"They wouldn't want us as witnesses to Blackstone's seeds, either. They wanted to corner the market on a multi-million-dollar opportunity," Harry said.

"So, Knox killed Blackstone." Lila said. "And chased me away from the greenhouse – tried to kill me, too?"

"More likely, it was Knox's accomplice. Wormwood." Harry grit his teeth. "He had to be the main force behind all of it, from the beginning."

"You," Keaton looked at Lila, "should write a paper about all of this, about Blackstone's work. Something you can publish after we're done distributing the seeds."

Lila smiled. "Great idea. I can start on it now. But when do we want to tell people what we've done?"

"Wait 'till we've passed out all of the seeds except a few we keep for ourselves. Then, sister," Harry put his fingers on her arm, "you decide, anytime, after that."

A warmth passed from his hand into hers. "We'll

call the new variety Blackstone's chokecherry," she said, "and I'll plant two or three in the greenhouse he used."

"Hey, his original plant should still be there." Harry raised his finger.

"Would Wormwood have taken it?" Keaton asked.

"Maybe," Lila said. "But there are rows and rows of plants in there. Dr. Blackstone knew his own labeling system, but nobody else did. Wormwood would have to test them all to know which was the right one."

"Or take all of them," Keaton said.

"That's pretty unlikely. It's a crime scene, after all. The cops will probably be watching the place." Harry sipped his coffee. "Anyway, the seeds were the greater prize and now he thinks he has them."

"Right, that's right," she agreed. "I'll have time to test the bushes when we get back and find the mother plant. We should have a harvest of seeds from that one next year."

"Don't let the feds take that plant," Harry's voice deepened.

"Good point. Maybe I can hide it somewhere."

"Johnny can hide it for us," Harry said.

Keaton groaned.

"Well, he owes me…"

"My dear, dear friends." Lila patted each of them on the shoulder. "Big brothers, really…"

"Hey, that one's old enough to be your grandpa," Harry pointed to Keaton, who huffed.

"…it's time to hit the road again." She gave them a winning smile.

CHAPTER 57

They nurtured the Bel Air north along the Rocky Mountains, meeting friends and friends of friends, telling their tale, leaving three or four seeds with each person they thought they could trust. Lila mailed ten seeds to a friend in Toronto, with a note to hold onto them for her. When they had sixteen seeds left, they headed east again toward Indiana.

Once back in Bluejacket, Lila gave the mother plant and twelve of her seeds to Harry, who gave them to Johnny, who hid them among his cash crops.

Lila wrote an article announcing the discovery but omitting the fact that she and Keaton and Harry had already distributed hundreds of Dr. Blackstone's seeds to dozens of people who'd agreed to nurture plants of their own. And who'd agreed to keep quiet at least until after their first big harvest, which they also would send to like-minded citizens of the Earth.

Lila hired a lawyer and told her the whole story, all of it subject to the attorney-client privilege. After two days of confidential negotiations, the USCIS decided not to revoke her student visa.

Then she gave her last four seeds to Mr. Jones, who immediately seized Dr. Blackstone's research and all of the two dozen perfectly normal chokecherry bushes from the greenhouse. The Department of Agriculture and Department of Homeland Security began an investigation which they kept confidential, at least until the attorney released Lila's article to the Washington Post.

The FBI investigated the death of Dr. Blackstone and eventually arrested Franny Knox, Keith Wormwood, and his associates for murder, attempted murder, theft, fraud, and conspiracy to commit each of those and other associated crimes, all while crossing multiple state lines. She, Keaton, and Harry told their story to whoever inquired, invoking the Fifth Amendment protection against self-incrimination whenever asked what specifically caused them to be at the abandoned rancheria in the desert east of El Paso.

Neville remains wanted for assault with a deadly weapon and attempted kidnapping. Police confiscated his cache of M-16s, grenades, pistols, and knives and collapsed his partial tunnel to the stockpile.

Harry booked himself and Keaton on two national talk shows. Keaton used some of his fees from the shows to open an antique furniture repair shop in Bluejacket.

Harry used his money to invest in legitimate agricultural research companies and to open a used bookstore he called Blackstone's Books. The store occupies the main floor of an old Spanish Colonial house. Keaton later moved his repair shop to the garage behind the home. Keaton and Harry now live in separate rooms on the second floor.

After brief posturing against the Department of Agriculture and Homeland Security, Lila was able to return to her classes the following spring semester, where she focused on genetic engineering.

The 1960 Bel Air remains comfortably parked in a garage behind Blackstone's Books and can be seen in the Fourth of July parade in Bluejacket and, on sunny days, cruising the country highways with its window wings open.

AUTHOR'S NOTE AND ACKNOWLEDGEMENTS

Thank you for reading The Antidote – I really hope you enjoyed it! As an author, I depend heavily on book reviews and referrals. If you think others might enjoy the novel, too, please leave a quick review on Amazon or any other internet site you use for selecting books to read. The moment it takes to leave a quick book rating makes a lasting difference for the author!

The potential for plants to become part of the antidote for radical climate change seems intuitive. Research into this approach has been on-going, but our propensity to fight over shrinking resources or cultural differences can divert essential energy from the task. We must learn to regulate ourselves so that future generations may survive.

I hope The Antidote sparks some thought about where our next breakthrough might occur and the intense need for humans to reach solutions for the problems humans create. Our hard work and "big" brains got us into this mess. Now they need to get us out.

Hats off to my lovely and patient wife for all her support while working on this effort. Thanks to her, Dad, Sarah, and Julie for their valued insights and edits. Thanks to my friends, family, and colleagues, whose support helped keep my head above water.

I also want to thank my editor, Jim Dempsey, for his encouragement, careful attention to detail, and insightful suggestions. And I thank Daniel Thiede for his beautiful cover art and book design and his much-needed help with the technical aspects of the work.

Thanks to all who understand our kinship with the planet and those who work in the service of their ideals.

RAPTOR CANYON

The tent became a dome of light, then began to smolder and burst into flame near the back, near the kitchen stove.

"Hey, we just cleaned the grill back there," Relic said, making Wyatt laugh.

The fire spread slowly, casting a halo of light across the camp. Security guards hollered, workers yelled their curses and questions, and everyone rushed to see what the commotion was all about.

"Is she really crazy enough to do that?" Wyatt asked.

"Yep," Relic nodded.

"Well, shee-it," Wyatt did his best imitation of Faye.

Relic smiled. "Don't let her hear you or she'll knock your block off."

"No doubt."

"Would you see what you can do to slow down that backhoe up ahead of us and anything else with a lock and key? Then work your way north, swing back toward the staircase and we can meet up there."

Wyatt nodded.

"Keep a close look out. They'll be searching as soon as the mess is under control."

"What's your next move?" Wyatt asked.

Relic jerked his thumb toward the portable toilets.

"Really?" Wyatt said.

Relic turned and faded into the dark. Wyatt heard

footfalls, someone moving quickly toward him. After a moment, he recognized her shape bobbing along. She tossed something and he heard it clacking into the bed of a pickup. She nearly ran into him.

"Hey." He put his hands out toward her.

"Hey," she said, slowing, but only a bit. "Here." She tossed a stick of dynamite to him, the fuse sparkling lit.

"Shit!"

"Throw it!" she shouted as she ran past. "Now!"

Wyatt stared at the tube in his hand. The fuse sputtered and spat and shortened with every second, time compressed with the tightness of his breath, the glowing fuse moving forward immutably until something like a spinning clutch popped in his chest and muscle movement became possible again. He reached his arm back and threw it as far and as fast as he could, then he spun and ran to the side of another truck and turned back to look.

The pickup Faye had tossed something into rose into the air with a smack that washed away all other sound, then fell back to the ground with a nasty twist as pieces of sheet metal dropped from the sky.

"Holy…"

Wyatt's stick of dynamite exploded somewhere beyond another truck, lighting something on fire, sending a second sonic boom through his skull, making him jump in his tracks. He stared at the blaze as it settled into a steady burn and looked the direction Faye had run.

A third, fourth, and fifth explosion erupted in quick

succession in the row of portable toilets and Wyatt knew it was Relic's work. Where was Relic's peaceful resistance now? Lord, he hoped no one was in those toilets. Then, he thought, what a mess of shit, and he giggled and smacked his hands together.

Oh, my god, was it possible to have so much fun? He never expected stopping Lord Winnieship from stealing this canyon to feel so damn good.

He stared at the fire he'd started and tried to think. He wanted to follow Faye but there was no telling what other mayhem she had in mind, and he did not want to walk into an exploding outhouse. He tried to regulate his breathing, with only a little luck. He circled away from the path Faye had taken, giving her a wide berth, moving to the outer edge of the parked vehicles.

Wyatt turned and trotted toward a lone backhoe, maybe sixty yards away. Though the electric lights of the compound were out, the kitchen and dining room blaze cast a sallow glow on the tops of the other tents and equipment. The upper arm of the yellow backhoe was lit like a candle.

His shins scraped across brittle sage and he slowed to a walk. He'd lost his own toothpicks, so that trick would not work with the heavy equipment. After Faye's dynamite, toothpicks seemed pretty pathetic anyway. Maybe there was a set of keys kept in the ignition that he could toss away. Or maybe he could flatten its tires or pull wires from under the dash to disable the beast. He turned to watch the bobbing of flashlights all around the burning mess tent a quarter of a mile away. The voices of men rose and fell in a rhythm that was almost musical, like an offbeat composition.

He stopped at the base of the backhoe and stared up at the top, where the boom and dipper attached. He circled the machine to the open cabin and peered inside.

"Stop and turn around." The voice was deep and familiar.

Wyatt turned and raised his hands. Even in the semi-dark, Lynch's muscled bulk identified him immediately. He held a pistol aimed at Wyatt's chest.

"You!" Lynch said. "You sonofabitch."

Wyatt saw the left hook a milli-second before it struck his jaw, wrenching his head away and toward the ground. He stumbled to the side. A blow to his stomach struck like a rocket and his chest ached, all the veins in his body shut down by a sonic boom. Slivers of light flashed through his eyes, closed tight against the assault. He sensed himself floating to the earth, his muscles turned to liquid. He was out before he hit the dirt.

WINGS OVER
GHOST CREEK

He sucked a shallow breath of air, pulled his gaze from the dead arm, and looked back the way he'd come. From this perspective, the arm was well-hidden on the backside of the long pile of dirt, tucked close to the low rock face and well out of view from the hangar and the tents beyond. Last night's heavy storm had flushed loose soil from the canyon slopes and probably from the body, too. He tried not to look back at the fragile hand, but he couldn't help himself. Skin shriveled against the tiny bones, stiff leather holding the assembly of joints together, keeping the fingers pointed in confusing, haphazard directions, their owner not sure which way to go. Red nail polish added a cheap party flare, a celebration completely out of place.

Holy eff. Hold it together, he told himself, get back to camp and pretend he'd never seen it. Tell Thomas. No one else. Someone here could have killed this girl, must have killed her. Why? What had happened here?

He turned his eyes to his feet and shuffled across the ground, moving to the edge of the pile of dirt. He peered around the mound and saw the edge of the hangar and the back of the tents. No one seemed to be around, so he hustled away from the dirt, across the hard-packed surface, and into the hangar. He went to the yellow plane again and leaned on the right strut, his breath still shallow and labored.

Owen looked beyond the hangar to the field outside and the Cessna waiting for them. Where was Thomas?

"Did you get that cold drink?"

Panic charged through his brain, a devil's hot wire crackling from one ear to the other. His head jerked toward the front of the plane and he clamped his hands tightly on the strut. Everett's question was smooth but – was there an undertone in his voice?

Owen managed to force a breath.

"No…" he patted the wing support, glanced at Everett, then spoke to the plane itself, too nervous to look at the man again. Squeezing the strut helped him to focus. "I got sidetracked by this old Aeronca. What year is it, do you know?"

"1946, I'm told."

"Oh."

"Are you a pilot?" Everett moved out of the sunlight and into the shade of the hangar. Owen knew the man could see him better now.

"No, no, I'm not. Tried to take some lessons, but…" He struggled to keep his thoughts on the aircraft, away from what he'd discovered. "Just look at this panel, the instrument panel," he pointed. "Not hardly any instruments here, though. It's all metal, too, like the dashboards on old cars." He kept his eyes on the cockpit, still reluctant to look directly at Everett.

"Yeah, I've looked it over myself." Everett's voice

seemed more normal now, more conversational. "The owner has a friend who came out here a couple of days ago. He's restoring the old bird, but I don't know how far he's gotten. The fabric looks like a stiff breeze would pull it off." He ran his hand across the edge of the wing opposite Owen. "You wouldn't catch me flying in this death trap." Everett wandered away from the plane, plucked a long blade of grass from the ground and began to twist it absentmindedly.

"Yeah, the cloth on this one needs completely replaced." Owen tried to sound like an authority on the subject and felt his nerves calm a little as he spoke. He ducked under the wing and walked into the sunlight. "Seen my boss?"

"I think he's about done," Everett pointed toward the tents along Ghost Creek. Thomas and Angela were walking slowly back toward the Cessna. Angela was explaining something, Thomas nodding.

"Well, it was nice meeting you." Everett moved quickly toward Owen and offered his hand, his smile show-room friendly, his shake cold and curt.

"Yes. Nice meeting you, too." Owen made eye contact briefly and turned back toward the Cessna. "Better get going."

He strode toward the rented Park Service plane, muscle memory moving his legs, thoughts flowing back to that tortured hand, its ragged movement in the breeze. He tried to be nonchalant about getting the hell out of there. Angela and Thomas came closer to the Cessna.

"Got what we need?" Owen asked Thomas.

Thomas looked up. "Yep. Thanks for the tour and good luck to you," he said to Angela. He shook hands with her and Everett and turned back to the plane.

Owen did not wait to be told to climb in. He adjusted his seatbelt, put the headset on, and waited. Thomas did the same.

How was he going to tell Thomas about the dead girl's arm? When should he tell him? Angela and Everett positioned themselves to one side and in front of the Cessna. They could see any conversation between him and Thomas, so he stayed quiet.

Thomas spent a moment examining the air map and checking the instruments. Out of the corner of his eye, Owen saw the man with the red hat, Luke, run up to Everett and whisper urgently in his ear. Everett glared at the plane, then gave some sort of order to Luke, who ran out of view. Did they know he'd found the girl's body?

"Clear prop!" Thomas pumped the throttle and turned the key, the engine spitting to life. Owen sat back in his seat, eyes straight ahead, and listened to the engine as Thomas adjusted the fuel mixture and checked the magnetos, turning first one off, then the other, then both back on for flight, Owen wishing he would hurry the hell up. Thomas finally pushed the throttle forward and the engine roared, the Cessna shuddered, and they began to roll down the dirt strip, vibrating, bouncing, jarring over small ruts until suddenly, liftoff, and the ride became smooth and even, the engine solid and throaty, clear air ahead of them, and Owen finally took a deep breath.

Thomas made a gentle turn to their left, flying back toward the creek, the dig site, and the old hangar, circling to gain altitude needed to fly over the plateau above the camp. They rose steadily as they went, Owen thinking how to explain what he'd found, hoping he'd done the right thing by waiting until they were in the air, bound for home base.

They leveled out about two miles past the Quonset hut, aiming for the broad Colorado River as they continued to climb beyond the canyon. A ribbon of dust rose to their right, a truck in motion along the road, soon to be well behind them. Ghost Creek faded from view as they neared the level of the plateau. They could see the bronze river beyond as it wound its way southward, on toward the Grand Canyon, on to the Gulf of California. Owen rubbed his hands on his pants and readied himself.

"Thomas," he spoke into the microphone on his headset.

"Yes?"

"I've got something to tell you, something I discovered down there while you were with the archeologist..."

"Yes?" Thomas checked his GPS and adjusted his heading.

Just then, a hollow thump jarred Thomas forward and he pushed the yoke in, then tugged and released it as he slumped back in his seat. Owen grabbed the yoke and his eyes swelled wide and he stared at Thomas' slackened face and began to scream his name, bobbing the plane's nose up, down, up, when another hollow thump jarred them and oil sprayed into the air and onto the right side of the windshield and he heard the motor cough, and cough again, and felt the Cessna lose its power, dropping in the air, descending toward the ground and he screamed again.

DIAMONDS OF DEVIL'S TAIL

"Wicked chickens lay deviled eggs, but this one's rotten, too." Relic took the binoculars from his eyes and stroked his buffalo-beard goatee. Something about the man on the trail below made his skin tingle.

He slid away from the edge, out of the man's line of sight, and looked about. An unlikely descendant from clans of the Hopi and Scottish, Relic wandered the remote reaches of the Green and Colorado Rivers and the high plateaus between them, a weathered hermit at home in the desert outback, roaming ancient trails, brewing his homemade gin at a couple of narrow, spring-fed crags tucked above the floodplains. He tightened his ponytail, errant strands of white flashing through his coal-black hair.

A dried-out branch of cottonwood leaned against the nearest in a row of six Pueblo houses nestled tightly between the floor and ceiling of the cliff, a string of separate rooms, their stone blocks still mortared together in the corners. Inside were mano stones, held in the hand for grinding corn, and metate, wide-bottom slabs used for the same purpose. A child's bow and arrow, chert for making knives and arrowheads, and bowls of corn, squash, and other seeds were set neatly on indoor ledges under a layer of dust; their owners, it seemed, only away for the winter. In the farthest room was a row of large pots painted with white and black bolts of lightning, edges curved and sharp, with handles on their sides, tops still sealed tight, their contents a thousand year-old mystery. Relic meant to keep it that way.

He leaned forward again. The man strode purposefully toward the high cliff with something long, something strangely out of place, glinting in the desert sun. He put the binoculars back to his eyes.

Of all the things to be lugging in this remote country, to be balancing on bony shoulders in the noonday heat, that angular, outrageous shape was an aluminum ladder, designed for the suburban handyman.

"Well, shit on a shingle." Relic tucked the binoculars away, lay flat near the ruins, and waited.

The man struggled awkwardly up the trail, finally dragging the extension ladder to a stop at the base of the sandstone cliff. He wiped the sweat from his forehead and gazed upward at the solid, sloping rock and the extreme measures the Pueblo people had taken to keep their houses and granaries hidden and safe, high in the cliffs and crags, deep in the desert outback. Centuries ago, they carried masonry, mortar, and jars of water up rickety, wooden ladders to build these solid structures; hard, hot work with just one purpose – protection against interlopers. Now the man below had a ladder of his own, and he rested it against the stone and tugged on the rope that extended it upward, the arms squealing in their tracks, each rung clunking into place as it went.

The man shifted an empty duffle bag across his shoulders and began climbing carefully, one step at a time.

The twenty-eight foot ladder shifted suddenly an inch to the side, but it seemed to find a new, more solid base. The man flexed his knees, testing to make sure the aluminum would not slide any farther, and glanced up. The top of the ladder reached just above the lip of the sandstone ledge.

That man must think he'll find a load of artifacts up here, Relic thought, maybe even lower them to the ground by rope from the ruins, then step back down the ladder unencumbered. But the ancient Pueblo had one last line of defense.

Relic rolled away from the ruins and shifted along the ledge until he was directly in front of the top rung of the ladder, waiting. He listened as the man placed one hand on the step above him, then the next, one at a time, rising cautiously higher.

The man reached the cap of the ledge, but when he looked across the level shelf, where the stone walls rested, there, alone in the red dust, sat Relic looking, he knew, like a weathered Pueblo man, a ghost of the ruins, with a black goatee and a ponytail, holding a three foot cottonwood branch as thick as his arm.

"Shit!" the man's foot slid off one rung and down to the next. "Holy mother...who the hell are you?"

Relic's dark eyes squinted, his lips rose at the corners, and he slid the branch toward the man's ladder.

"What the hell?" the man tightened his grip.

Relic placed the branch on the top rung and began to push.

"No! Shit, no!" He raised his hand for a flash then returned it to the ladder. "You'll kill me!"

Relic slowly pushed the ladder away from the ledge, forcing it to twist outward on one end, then the other, as it lifted from the face of the cliff.

The man dropped both feet to the lower rung and slid his hands quickly down the aluminum sides, dropping his feet, holding for a moment, dropping, holding, dropping as the ladder leaned farther and farther away from the cliff, more and more upright above, ready to catapult him into a pile of rocks, and just as his feet hit the dirt the ladder tipped past its balance, dipped overhead and spun out of his hands and onto the rocky ground with a clang, a bounce, and another clang!

BROKEN INN

"Well, butter my buns…"

He shaded his eyes with the palm of his hand.

There were two pickup trucks in Demon's Roost canyon – one in the deep arroyo at the base of sheer cliffs to the south, one on the upper flats that made up most of the corkscrew canyon. There'd been uranium mining here in the 1950s, but what these yahoos were doing now was a mystery.

Relic tightened his ponytail and stared into the twisting gorge.

Yesterday morning, snow capped the hoodoos – white icing on scarlet cupcakes. By this afternoon, the sun-fired rocks had begun radiating heat near 100 degrees, wringing moisture from the human body like a twisted sponge. The cliffs above him seemed to glow, slivers of clay injected into the blood-red sandstone like fat marbled into raw steak. A pair of crows squawked overhead.

An unlikely descendent of disparate clansmen – one Scottish, one Hopi – Relic wandered these plateaus and chasms, a sometimes-trespasser, recluse, and moonshiner. He'd been called a vagabond, a sasquatch of the desert, but these remote places were home.

He left his pack by a rock and trotted down the trail to the bottom of the canyon. He moved quickly around the first bend to a spot close to the truck on the flats. No one seemed to be around. He walked to the pickup, a silver double-cab, its tailgate down. Topographic maps lay flattened across the truck bed, rocks on the corners to hold them in place. An empty five-gallon container for water sat on the end of the tailgate, neon-orange stripes across its side. A gust of wind slid the plastic canister off the edge and Relic picked it up.

The maps were of Demon's Roost and places to the north. Scribbles and circles were penciled over the contour lines, but he couldn't tell what they meant. The second truck, the one in the dry creek bed, sat around a bend in the canyon, out of sight from this position.

Something made him uneasy. Some distant vibration, maybe. The crows had gone silent. Charcoal clouds hung in the east.

Two men rounded the corner, boots rasping over the sand, heads down, mumbling to each other. He watched from behind the silver truck, some fifteen feet above them and thirty yards away. One wore jeans and a white dress shirt, out of place in this remote canyon. The other wore a red shirt with a leather strap across his shoulder.

Relic took a step back and felt it again – this time a deep rumble under his boots – and suddenly he knew what was coming. Though desperately dry, it was water that had shaped these desert lands, sheer bluffs and jagged drainages wrought by the power of rain. A cloudburst 50 miles away could become a flash flood in these narrow canyons, a deadly blast of water exploding with little warning. The men in the arroyo stood directly in its path.

"Hey, hey!" Relic raised the empty water container above his head, waving it in the air, sprinting past the pickup truck and toward the edge of the ravine.

One of the men looked up.

"Get out of there! Out of there!" Relic shouted, pointing up the embankment, urging them to run from the dry creek bed before it was too late.

The other man straightened, suddenly startled, and reached for his side.

"Flash flood! Flash flood!" Relic waved the plastic canister again and stepped to the edge of the ravine.

The dissonance in his toes became a bellow in his head, an angry groan.

One man began to climb from the bottom of the arroyo, boots slipping up the sandy rise. The other lifted his hand from his side, a pistol in his fingers, aiming it toward Relic.

Relic spiraled backward reflexively, stepping suddenly into thin air, dropping down the slope, skidding feet-first through loose sand all the way to the bottom. He stood and looked at the gunman, who'd holstered his pistol and begun climbing the side of the arroyo behind his companion. In a moment, they both stood above the empty drainage, out of danger.

Now the sound of thunder rolled through the canyon, echoes doubling the alarm. Relic ran down the dry bed, frantically searching its steep walls for a place he could ascend. The rumble became the roar of whitewater, ramjet engines at full throttle, all other sound blasted aside by the urgency and enormity of the coming flood.

Relic turned in time to see a two-foot bank of water rise behind him, precursor to the deluge to come.

He held tight to the empty container and ran toward the spot the two men had used to climb from the dry bed, but as he began to scramble up the slope, the coffee-colored water, heavy with silt, reached his feet, sweeping them forward, twisting him down into the roiling river.

He wrapped his arms around the canister, his make-shift life vest, and lifted his feet in front of him. A surge forced him underwater – his eyes closed, mouth shut – then lifted him rapidly toward the top of the arroyo, shoving him forward faster than a man could run. He kicked to keep his feet downstream, buffers against rocks, trees, or cliffs. The newborn river hurtled him around the bend, a choleric infant wailing at the world.

The second pickup truck lay directly in his path.

He wiggled and twisted, paddling his boots as fast as he could, but the truck came swiftly closer, closer, his feet about to smash into the rear window. If he were forced through the glass and into the cab of the truck, the river would pin him there and drown him. But as he approached, he seemed to slow, then slow some more. His boots touched the window. He bent his knees and pushed away, then he realized he hadn't slowed at all. The truck had been lifted from the ground and shoved forward with him. The water carried them both through the flood together.

The deluge raged around another bend in the canyon, rocks clacking violently against each other along the bottom, tumbling into the flow from the sides, debris that could crush him in a second if he got caught between them. The truck separated from him, rolling to its side. A wave suddenly tossed his head and chest above the flow, his feet pulled downward. He flipped forward and under the rapids, no time to take a breath. Despite the buoyancy of the canister, the swirling river forced him downward, somersaulting into the dark. He lost all sense of direction, what was up or down, dizzy in the swirling storm, helpless under the unyielding, raging current. Pressure rose in his lungs to near explosion, his diaphragm tensing, preparing to blow his final breath from his chest, when finally he spun upward, his head breaking through, and he gasped.

He pushed on the container, lifting his head as high as he could, hungrily sucking in air. The sides of the arroyo sped by, bending left, then right, disorienting him. His boots struck something hard, and he realized his legs were dangling below him again – a dangerous position. He pulled himself into a back float, feet downstream, arms clutching the canister. Waves splashed into his eyes and mouth, blinding him for seconds at a time, forcing him to take quick, shallow breaths. The current threatened to spin him again, so he paddled his feet, twisting to keep his face above water.

The waves began to spread farther apart and his sight improved when he squinted. The truck was behind him now, spinning slowly in the current as he passed another bend in the gorge.

The sky seemed to lighten as the canyon walls receded. He felt his elevation lower as the flood spread across more open ground, closer to its destination in the Colorado River.

He spun to his left and kicked as hard as he could, moving out of the current. In moments, his bottom touched hard ground. He pushed farther away from the receding water until he could sit up. A three-inch flow continued to swirl around him, but he knew he was safe.

He took full, deep breaths, clearing the adrenaline from his system, regaining a sense of balance.

The flow of water slowly turned to mud. The truck had rounded the last corner, then gotten stuck behind a rock and buried nearly a foot deep in the sandy bottom. He dropped the empty container and wiped the water and hair from his eyes.

"This is the worst thing that's happened since the last thing," he told himself with a grin. It was the second time he'd been caught in a flash flood and nearly drowned. The first time, it'd been his own damn fault. Well, hell, he thought, maybe it was his own fault this time, too.

If the swim hadn't been so deadly, part of him, at least, could have admitted to the thrill.

He sat for a moment, staring into the clear sky. Who were those guys and what the hell were they doing in this canyon? And why did one of them draw his pistol when he'd warned them about the flood?

"I guess no good deed goes unpunished," he scolded himself. He stood slowly, shaking out his arms and legs. He removed his shirt, wrung it out, and put it back on. "I'll dry you out later," he spoke to his pants and boots.

It was time to get the hell out of there.

Sign up for book announcements and special deals at:

AWBALDWIN.COM

Also available from Award Winning Author
A.W. Baldwin:

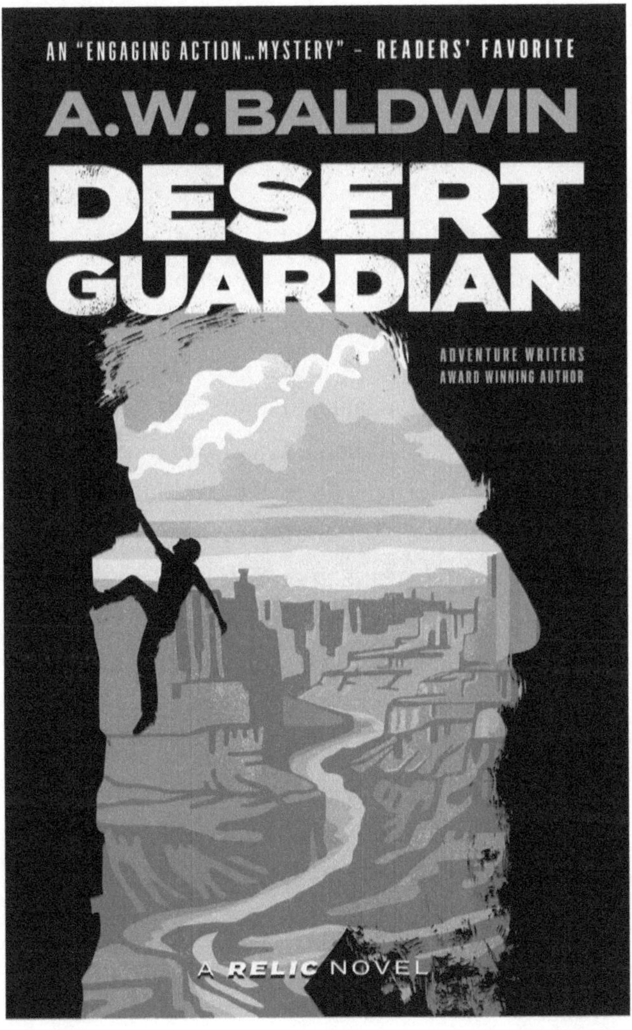
AN "ENGAGING ACTION...MYSTERY" - READERS' FAVORITE
A.W. BALDWIN
DESERT
GUARDIAN
ADVENTURE WRITERS
AWARD WINNING AUTHOR
A RELIC NOVEL

A moonshining hermit.
A campus bookworm.
A midnight murder.

Ethan's world turns upside-down when he slips off the edge of red-rock cliffs into a world of twisting ravines and coveted artifacts. Saved by a mysterious desert recluse named Relic, Ethan must join a whitewater rafting group and make his way back to civilization. But someone in the gorge is killing to protect their illegal dig for ancient treasures... When Anya, the lead whitewater guide, is attacked, he must divert the killer into the dark canyon night, but his most deadly pursuer is not who he thinks... Ethan struggles to save his new friends, face his own mortality, and unravel the chilling murders. But when they flee the secluded canyon, a lethal hunter is hot on their trail…

Can an unlikely duo and a whitewater crew save themselves and an ancient Aztec battlefield from deadly looters?

Readers' Favorite says:
Desert Guardian is an "engaging action… mystery"
The novel features "tough, credible characters"
Readers' Favorite Five Star Review

Buy now from a bookstore near you or amazon.com

A.W. BALDWIN

RAPTOR CANYON

GRANDMASTER
AWARD
FINALIST

A *RELIC* NOVEL

A moonshining hermit.
A big-city lawyer.
A $35million con job.

An impromptu murder leads a hermit named Relic to an unlikely set of dinosaur petroglyphs and to swindlers using the unique rock art to turn the canyon into a high-end tourist trap. Attorney Wyatt and his boss travel to the site to approve the next phase of financing, but his boss is not what he seems... When a treacherous security chief tries to kill Relic, Wyatt is caught in the deadly chase. The mismatched pair must tolerate each other while fleeing through white-water rapids, remote gorges, and hidden caverns. Relic devises a plan to save the treasured canyon, but Wyatt must come to terms with the cost to his career if he fights his powerful boss... A college student with secret ties to the site, Faye joins the kitchen crew so she can spy on the enigmatic project. When she hears Relic's desperate plan, she has a decision to make...

Armed with a full box of toothpicks (and a little dynamite), can the unlikely trio monkey-wrench the corrupt land deal and recast the fate of Raptor Canyon?

"A gem of a read..."
– *Dirk Cussler, #1 New York Times best-selling author*

"[You'll be] holding your heart and your breath at the same time…"
– *Peter Greene, award winning author of The Adventures of Jonathan Moore series*

"A hoot of an adventure novel…"
– *Reader's Favorite, Five Star Review.*

** Grand Master Adventure Writer's Finalist Award **

** Screencraft Cinematic Book Contest Semi-finalist **

Buy now from a bookstore near you or amazon.com

"A RETURN OF THE MYSTERIOUS HERMIT RELIC... A PAGE-TURNING THRILLER" - DIRK CUSSLER
A.W. BALDWIN
WINGS OVER GHOST CREEK
ADVENTURE WRITERS AWARD WINNING AUTHOR
ADVENTURE WRITERS COMPETITION FINALIST 2020
A RELIC NOVEL

A moonshining hermit.
A reluctant pilot.
A $5million plunder.

Owen discovers a murdered corpse at a college-run archeological dig in the Utah outback but when he and a park service pilot try to reach the sheriff for help, their plane is shot from the sky. Owen must ditch the aircraft in the Colorado River, where he is saved by a gin-brewing recluse named Relic. The offbeat pair flee from the sniper and circle back to warn the students but not everyone there is who they seem... The two must trek through rugged canyon country, unravel a baffling mystery, and foil a remarkable form of thievery. Suzy, a student at the dig, helps spearhead their escape but the unique team of crooks has a surprise for them...

Can they uncover the truth and escape an archeology field class that hides assassins and dealers in black-market treasure?

"A beautifully written thriller."
– *Readers' Favorite Five Star Review*

"[A] humorous, fun, and well-plotted adventure. Baldwin is a master storyteller..."
– Landon Beach, Bestselling Author of *The Sail*

"Baldwin delivers another gripping Relic tale with trade-mark wit and deft expression. This is adventure with philosophy that keeps you nodding your head long after you've put the book down."
– Jacob P. Avila, *Cave Diver*, Grand Master Adventure Writers Award Winner

Wings offers "…action-packed adventure and nerve-racking suspense, with a touch of romance and humor mixed in." Baldwin has a "gift for capturing the reader's attention at the beginning and keeping them spellbound"
– *Onlinebookclub.org* review

*** Grand Master Adventure Writer's Finalist Award ***

*** Screencraft Cinematic Book Contest Semi-finalist ***

Buy now from a bookstore near you or amazon.com

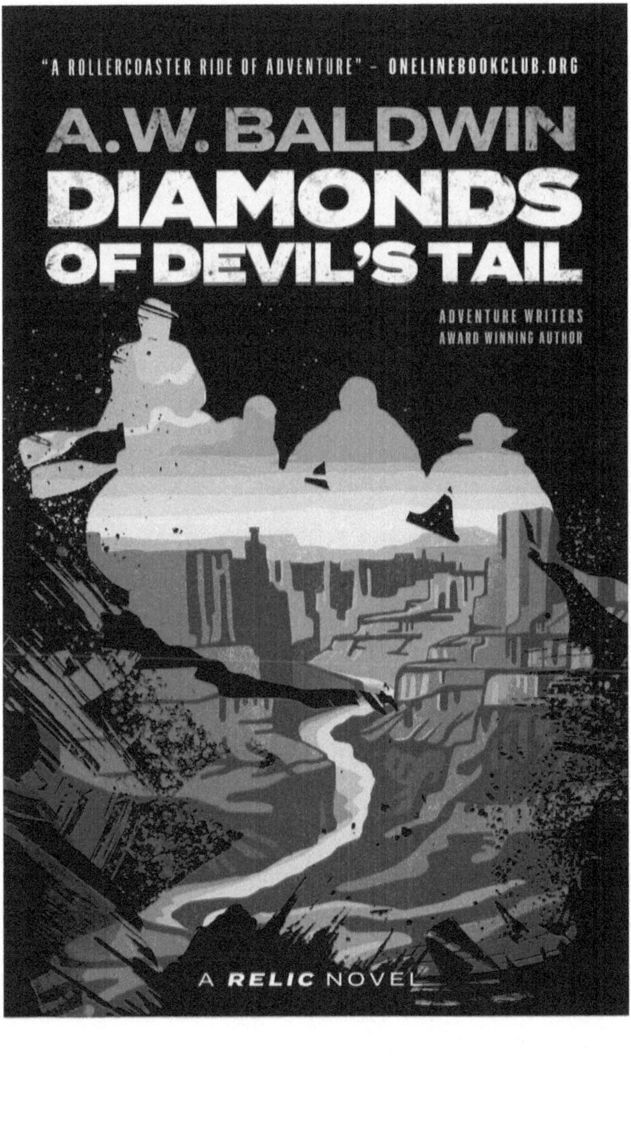
"A ROLLERCOASTER RIDE OF ADVENTURE" - ONELINEBOOKCLUB.ORG
A.W. BALDWIN
DIAMONDS OF DEVIL'S TAIL
ADVENTURE WRITERS AWARD WINNING AUTHOR
A RELIC NOVEL

A moonshining hermit.
An English major.
A $4 million jewel heist.

When diamonds appear in a remote canyon stream, whitewater rafters and artifact thieves set off in a deadly race to the source.

Brayden, an aspiring writer, works in a Chicago insurance firm with his ambitious uncle when they embark on a wilderness whitewater adventure. On a remote hike, they find their colleague, Dylan, dead in the sand, a handful of gems in his fist. When thieves charge in, Brayden flees deeper into the canyon, where he encounters a gin-brewing recluse named Relic. Brayden's uncle is cornered and cuts a deal with the thieves, but they each have a surprise for the other... and the rafters have ideas of their own about getting rich quick... Brayden and Relic must become allies, traverse the harsh desert, and beat the thieves to the hidden gems. Brayden must confront his uncle about suspicious payments at their insurance firm and what he was really doing at the stream where Dylan was killed...

Can they discover the truth, find the lost jewels, and protect the rafters from grenade-tossing thieves?

"…an adeptly written thriller…the excitement and tension are superb…the entire plot [is] compelling"
– *Readers' Favorite Five Star Review*

"straightforward and thrilling, with humor intermixed… Relic is a unique and intriguing character…passionately interested in preserving the ancient archeological sites and conserving the land and water…[We] enthusiastically recommend it to readers who enjoy thrillers, action-packed adventure, and crime novels."
– *Onlinebookclub.org* four out of four Star Review

"Another rollicking Relic ride from A.W. Baldwin…a bunch of double-crossing, dirt dealing, diamond thieves run into Relic's trademark wit and ingenuity. Enjoy!"
– Jacob P. Avila, *Cave Diver*, Grand Master Adventure Writers Award Winner

Buy now from a bookstore near you or amazon.com

A.W. BALDWIN

BROKEN INN

ADVENTURE WRITERS
AWARD WINNING AUTHOR

A *RELIC* NOVEL

A moonshining hermit
A budding reporter
A $25 million misdirection

The mob, undercover agents, and secret payloads make Broken Inn a dangerous place for a fresh reporter, a newspaper photographer, and a moonshining hermit.

Hailey witnesses a murder at the enigmatic Broken Inn, but when she learns that the hotel manager and her editor are pals, she investigates on her own. When a corrupt guard finds her snooping, she flees into a box canyon, where she is saved by a gin-brewing recluse named Relic. She reports the murder to a deputy, but for some reason, no arrests are made... She enlists help from Ash, the newspaper's photographer, but they must flee for their lives into the back country with Relic and a four-legged stray with a nose for trouble. They discover mysterious metal drums hidden deep in an abandoned uranium mine, but can't tell what's inside. And just when they're most desperate for help, they learn that not everyone is who they seem...

Can they uncover the secrets of Broken Inn, dodge the syndicate, and head off an environmental disaster?

"Danger scorches in another outstanding mystery by A.W. Baldwin"

– New York Times #1 Bestselling author Dirk Cussler

"Brilliantly executed… heart stopping excitement"

– Readers' Favorite Five Star Review

Grand Master Adventure Writer's Finalist Award

New York City Big Book Award – Distinguished Favorite

Global Book Awards

Independent Press Award – Distinguished Favorite

Books Shelf Award – Second Place

Buy now from a bookstore near you or amazon.com

www.ingramcontent.com/pod-product-compliance
Lightning Source LLC
Chambersburg PA
CBHW030800210726
48290CB00002B/357